Y0-ELK-457

The Doctor's Affair

ALSO BY ELIZABETH SEIFERT

Young Doctor Galahad
(Winner of $10,000 Prize)
A Great Day
Thus Doctor Mallory
Hillbilly Doctor
Bright Scalpel
Army Doctor
Surgeon in Charge
A Certain Doctor French
Bright Banners
Girl Intern
Doctor Ellison's Decision
Doctor Woodward's Ambition
Orchard Hill
Old Doc
Dusty Spring
So Young, So Fair
Take Three Doctors
The Glass and the Trumpet
The Strange Loyalty of
Dr. Carlisle
Hospital Zone
The Bright Coin
Homecoming
The Story of Andrea Fields
Miss Doctor
Doctor of Mercy
The Doctor Takes a Wife
The Doctor Disagrees
Lucinda Marries the Doctor
Doctor at the Crossroads
Marriage for Three
A Doctor in the Family
Challenge for Dr. Mays
A Doctor for Blue Jay Cove
A Call for Dr. Barton
Substitute Doctor
The Doctor's Husband
The New Doctor
Love Calls the Doctor
Home-Town Doctor
Doctor on Trial
When Doctors Marry
The Doctor's Bride
The Doctor Makes a Choice
Dr. Jeremy's Wife
The Honor of Dr. Shelton
The Doctor's Strange Secret
Legacy for a Doctor
Dr. Scott, Surgeon on Call
Katie's Young Doctor
A Doctor Comes to Bayard
Doctor Samaritan
Ordeal of Three Doctors
Hegerty, M.D.
Pay the Doctor
The Rival Doctors
Doctor with a Mission
To Wed a Doctor
The Doctor's Confession
Bachelor Doctor
For Love of a Doctor
A Doctor's Two Lives
Doctor's Kingdom
Doctor in Judgement
The Doctor's Second Love
Doctor's Destiny
The Doctor's Reputation
The Two Faces of Dr. Collier
The Doctor's Private Life
The Doctor's Daughter
Doctor in Love
Four Doctors, Four Wives

THE DOCTOR'S AFFAIR

Elizabeth Seifert

DODD, MEAD & COMPANY, New York

Printed in the United States of America

Library of Congress Cataloging in Publication Data

Seifert, Elizabeth, date
The doctor's affair.

I. Title.
PZ3.S4603Dqj [PS3537.D352] 813'.5'2 75-29218
ISBN 0-396-07202-X

The Doctor's Affair

PROLOGUE

It is, largely, a commuter flight, originating in late afternoon at the Denver airport, picking up and depositing travelers at Salt Lake City, and Boise, and terminating at Spokane in time for a drink before bedtime. It is popular, and, from frequent previous trips, the passengers know each other, know the attendants, and are courteously curious about strangers. I was one of those, and was quite willing to state my reason for being on the flight. I would be visiting my son's family to help them celebrate the confirmation of a grandson.

I liked the mountains, I liked the people who lived and worked in the thin, clean air. I listened eagerly, and watched, and formed small fantasies about some of the people I saw, using first impressions, scraps of talk, to build conclusions which I knew were ridiculous.

And I went completely overboard about the tall girl who boarded at the last split second before the plane left Salt Lake. The door had begun to close, and there were shouts, a gay young voice saying, "Wait for me!" and she popped through the reopened door, laughing, breathless, tossing her honey-colored hair back from her face. "Didn't you know I was coming?" she demanded, smiling brilliantly at the stewardess.

"I knew you were coming, Gretchen," said the young woman, "but I couldn't guess when."

This drew laughter from the men up and down the aisle, and the tardy passenger consented to take a seat behind me and fasten her seat belt.

I call her "girl" but she was a woman in her late twenties, I felt sure. I was sure, too, that she was a stunner. Tall, well-built—"cool" in the full sense of the word. Self-confidence rang in her clear voice and showed itself in the way she walked. I knew that she would be an excellent dancer. Those long-legged, supple-waisted women always are. People liked her, one could tell that.

And of course I became more and more interested in her, and regretted the brief time I would have to study her. She had come aboard carrying only one of those bright tote bags; she was wearing a tailored cotton dress, with a sweater hung across her shoulders; she would be getting off at Boise.

I was tempted to follow her. She carried a kind of excitement with her. This would reach any man, I thought, age not making very much difference. I had seen the same electric charge in skilled actresses, in singers. And of course in tramps on bar stools around the world.

And here it was in the person of a young woman with thick, shining gold hair, a stirring voice, a laugh that made anyone smile, and a manner that told each one of us that she liked us, that she was thrilled to be among us.

She greeted her Reuben sandwich with genuine pleasure. I had had mine before we touched down at Salt Lake. "I'm starved," she told the stewardess. "Could I just have 7Up instead of coffee? This is *good!* Where do you find your rye bread?"

It was good rye bread, but she made it special even in retrospect.

She chattered to others around her, especially to her seat mate, an older woman who evidently knew her well. And I frankly listened. Eagerly listened. Between eating her Reuben and answering those who passed her seat, she told her companion that she had spent the day shopping.

"Oh, I know I should stay with the home stores," she confessed. "Ida B. thinks I do."

Her companion said something.

"Of course she's not in business any more. And we never were very good customers—she had no idea of the value of simplicity. There never was a costume but what Ida B. draped it with scarves, pinned it with a huge rhinestone pin, and embellished it with strings of junk jewelry. And now— Do you know that woman is ninety-five? And her niece— Oh, my goodness *gracious!* Both of them crashing bores! But they give parties, so they are invited to parties. I avoid them when I can, but since they live on the town's only street . . ."

She laughed happily at what must have been a protest from the older woman. "Oh, dear, yes!" she agreed. "I do know that our town has grown! I do know that it never felt the depression of the thirties. Don't you suppose my father recites that litany every morning at breakfast, and before going to bed at night?

"Well, he almost does. But the truth is, nothing ever

happens. Nothing ever has happened in Idaho, darling!"

The stewardess came for the trays, and I could hear the rustle of paper behind me. "Look what I bought today," the young woman was saying. "No, darling, it is not a tablecloth." Again that lovely laughter rippled. "Look! I'll show you!" And she was out in the aisle, dropping folds of green and gold cloth over her head, fastening it tightly around her waist, letting the rich drapery settle about her feet. In an exaggeration of the fashion model's slump, she walked up and down the aisle, retorting to the comments made, thanking those who admired her. Even with the blue chambray of her dress blouse, the costume was fetching. I said as much to *my* neighbor, who nodded. "That girl," he agreed. "She can't claim nothing ever happens when she's around."

I was ready to pursue the point, and maybe get a question or two answered, when the stewardess came up behind the young woman who was telling one of the passengers just how much such a skirt cost by the square inch.

"Doctor," said the attendant, "there's a passenger sick in the rear of the plane. Could you . . . ?" And to my amazement, my girl had the stewardess help her out of the long skirt, and she was up the aisle, briskly, capably.

I sat bemused. All the beginnings of my imagination were flying behind us. That girl a *doctor?* Incredible!

It just couldn't be. It didn't—it didn't *fit!*

I began to gather the bits and pieces of what I did know about the woman. Her appearance, her impact, those were facts. Her gaiety and even impudence were there, too. People liked her. I liked her.

So—why wasn't she a doctor?

Because she didn't look like one? Because she didn't sound like one? And just how, I sternly asked myself, is a doctor supposed to look and sound?

Did he have to be a slightly stooped man, one with a clipped white mustache, and probably a balding head? He would say, "Hmmmnnn" in a considering tone of voice . . .

I snorted and opened the newspaper which I had bought in Denver. I was disappointed to have my girl taken away from my observance of her. I resisted the temptation to ask the stewardess what was going on in the rear of the plane.

And my forbearance was rewarded. We were preparing to descend over the brown mountains and the gleaming lakes, when the "doctor" returned to her seat, a little breathless. She thanked her seat companion for folding the long skirt and putting it into her bag. Was her billfold there? Yes, it was. Good!

"I'll tell you," she promised, "if I ever find the end of this blasted seat belt. Oh, there it is! All right." She lifted her voice slightly, knowing that we all of us were leaning forward to hear.

"There was this old lady," she said, "in distress. Evidently she had had a light stroke. I had the pilot ask for an ambulance to meet us. She can be taken to our hospital . . ." She paused. Then in answer to someone's remark or question, she said, "Oh, yes. Sure it's a good hospital. And we have good doctors!"

I couldn't decide if she worked at the "good hospital." Not from the way she spoke. She left the plane, as all the passengers did, through the boarding lounge. I had seen the ambulance waiting, but her "old lady" must have been taken to it through the rear door and a ramp. I saw no more of the beautiful young doctor, but I spent the rest of my trip, and some time after that, speculating about her. Wondering what her life was like.

As the passengers had gone along the aisle, I had heard someone ask who she was.

"Gretchen Purser," she was answered in a tone that assumed everyone knew Gretchen. "Her dad is Hugh Purser. She's married now, of course."

"Oh," said the first voice. "Of course. I knowed I knewed her, but I couldn't rightly call her name. She's growed, hasn't she?"

So! I gazed at the gray bulkhead of the plane, and arranged my thoughts. My girl was named Gretchen, her family were notable people, her dad's name was to be recognized. She was, incredibly, a doctor. She was beautiful, young, and popular. My eyes, my senses, told me that all these things were facts. What more did I need to know?

Well—she was known, she was popular. But was she liked? There was a distinction. Did she work at her profession? Was she married? Did she have children?

I wanted to know those things. I wanted to know each detail about this vibrant young woman. I wanted to know what her life was, what it had been, what it would be . . .

CHAPTER 1

THREE—perhaps as many as five—years before that plane trip on a June evening, Gretchen Purser was completing her four years of medical school. As she had infrequently done during those four years, Gretchen paused to wonder why she had ever entered medical school, why she had stuck with it. What would she do next? With an M.D. trailing her name, would life be different? It could be, but scarcely better.

Blessed with perfect health, strength, and enthusiasm, she was a smart and clever young woman, beautiful and lively.

She had been that four years ago when she might have done what her friends and schoolmates all were doing. Marrying, moving into attractive homes, producing a couple of beautiful children. Instead, what did Gretchen now have? Well, she had some white coats, some medical books—she would get her M.D., and probably her license.

And then what? Go home? Hardly. She would not leave this city, and Erwin Valier. He would not want her to. Both he and she expected her to stay, go into some office, hospital or clinic, and do some doctoring. *She* thought she would go into Valier's office, or even on his hospital service in some capacity. He was a staff doctor for the big teaching hospital, and an instructor. That was where he had met Gretchen, where she had met him. Where had begun the somewhat intense affair between them.

Valier was forty; Gretchen knew that. He was a handsome, virile man. His dark hair lay in crisp waves on his head, his face was classically handsome. He looked like a million dollars in hospital whites. His voice rang with assurance and authority. His patients adored him. He was married. Of course he was married. Gretchen knew that! But—so what?

A drink when they met by chance, a dinner together, several dinners. And then, a weekend. What harm?

The man had been attracted to her; for almost a year she had continued to interest him, to attract him. She felt confident that these same qualities would hold him. Very privately, she called it her *lure,* laughing at the term, but respecting what it meant to her. The mysterious power with which she seemed to be endowed. Her looks, her ability to interest people, to enjoy life. She didn't know just what the ingredients were. But if she kept herself presentable, had fun, things came her way. She could get almost anything she wanted, a certain room in a dormitory, a certain seat in the lecture hall—the demonstration desk in a lab—and dinner dates, a weekend, with Erwin Valier.

With few exceptions, ever since she had been aware of herself as a person—twelve, fifteen, certainly sixteen—

Gretchen had been able to have the things she wanted. A four-poster bed in her room at home, a short fur jacket, a convertible—and medical school. She thoroughly enjoyed the surprise, the shock, really, that people displayed when they met her and discovered . . .

Lure, charisma, charm, physical appeal—give it any name that might be lying about—Gretchen had used it throughout the four years of med school. She was intelligent enough to do the work for herself, but there were times—she could wheedle lecture notes to fill in for the day she took off to go horseback riding; she could always coax and secure covering for her hospital duties during her senior year. She hoped she had been able to make her victims like being victims. She wanted people to like her, and they generally did.

Since her charm worked with women as well as with men—almost as well—Gretchen had never considered it wrong to use her ability to please people. It certainly had got her out of a scrape or two, with no harm done that she could see. Who was hurt if she returned to the "hen coop" a little late? Well, two hours late, but what difference?

There were to be many times when Gretchen would wish that she had never gone on that weekend with Dr. Valier.

And yet, if she had not gone . . . And, after all, what a bust that had been! Simply, simply marvelous! He had got her back by bed check on Sunday night; it was her fault, though no wonder, that she missed the seven-thirty briefing on Monday morning. At the next session, the darned resident had chosen to question her in front of everyone. Students, interns, a nurse—the patient—and

Gretchen had been able to give him such outrageously funny replies, answers so evidently miles from the truth — Yes, she had had a big weekend. Well, not *big*. She had not spent much *money*. Well, yes, she had had company. Oh, he had said companions. That was different, wasn't it? Let's see— Unless the resident thought the case in hand that morning was more interesting . . . Nobody could learn a thing from her weekend. She had liked it all right, there were no duty calls, no notes to take or reports required. Why did everything in medical school have to be reported? Why?

Then, bless them, the resident spent the rest of the thirty minutes lecturing on the value of reports, their accuracy, their detail—

"Got away with it, didn't you, Gretch?" asked one of the other meds when they all had to go on to other duties, other classes, or even to eat breakfast.

"It wasn't too hard," said Gretchen, making her eyes wide and round.

She knew that she had got away with it. But since she had known that she could, through her cleverness, she had no regrets or guilt about the happening. She had enjoyed her weekend, and saw no reason to be penalized. She liked having fun much more than she did the many things she was supposed to do, like not being late for student briefings. She would do what she wanted to do! Let others step out of her way. If someone got hurt . . .

For instance, there had been that intern. His name was Butler and he wasn't anyone in particular. Just a guy . . .

Gretchen didn't even know if he liked her or not. It didn't matter. There had been the matter of intravenous feeding for a woman who had had surgery. She was not in critical condition, though she was in Recovery, of course, and the intern was in charge of several patients. He had asked a med student, who happened to be Gretchen, to keep an eye on the i.v. needle.

"Don't let her move her arm," he had said.

Gretchen nodded and sat down beside the bed. At first she had held the woman's arm, but her own arms and shoulders began to ache. She left the bedside for only a minute to ease her muscles, but the blasted patient must have moved . . .

Anyway, the glucose, or whatever, had gone into the tissues, the arm had swollen, got hard—all this was discovered after Gretchen had been relieved by a nurse and had gone elsewhere to do or observe other things.

There had been a great to-do over the whole thing. When the matter came up for staff discussion, the intern had not blamed her, but he did speak to her about it, as if he expected her to take the blame. Though *he* was the one in charge!

Of course it was too bad that he had lost preferential status over the matter. He blamed Gretchen, and her classmates blamed her. This created a pool of unpopularity which did disturb Gretchen. She wanted everyone to admire her, and she wished her classmates would, too. All of them. The patients did, the staff men—especially Dr. Valier.

Until—

It was just a week before graduation when he asked her what her plans were for the future.

All the senior meds were scheduled these final conferences with designated staff doctors. It was chance, purely, that required Gretchen to go to Dr. Valier's office, where she found him turning over the pages of her record folder.

"Things seem to be in pretty good shape, Gretchen," he said, leaning back in his chair. "What are your plans?"

She wanted small part of the impersonality bit. They were alone. Why couldn't she . . . ?

"What do *you* plan?" she asked pertly.

His face stiffened. "I'm not to be a feature in your plans, Gretchen," he said firmly.

She, too, stiffened. She was shocked, and for a split second she did not know what to do, or what to say. She had had no experience in feeling this way.

Of course she and Valier had not talked to each other about what came next; he had made no promises to her. She had asked for none.

"Well," she said now, "I'm glad my medical student status is about over. I am sure you felt it limited our relationship."

He met her gaze blankly, "Well, of course the teacher-student bit—"

She nodded and smiled. "Oh, that," she said in agreement. "But now, even if I work with you, things should be better."

He said nothing.

"Won't they?" she asked finally, to break the silence.

He looked at his watch, he closed her folder. "I don't know," he said.

Gretchen's fingertips stroked the side of her face; she hugged her arms across the front of her white coat. She was experiencing the strangest feeling. Was this man giving her the brushoff?

She asked him.

"Oh, no," he said quickly. "That isn't necessary. We'll be seeing each other. You are very good company, you know."

"But not good enough to work with?" she asked.

"Oh, well, you can see that wouldn't do, Gretchen." He rose and opened the hall door for her. He looked directly into her face. "Are you thinking that you are in love with me?" he asked curiously.

She straightened her shoulders. "I guess not," she said. "I wouldn't know about things of that sort," and she walked past him, hoping, *hoping* that she was carrying it off.

She had other assignments for the afternoon, but she walked down the corridor, she took the elevator, she walked out of the building. In love? She hadn't thought about that fine point.

But she had gone on that weekend; she had bought special clothes for it. She had been excited, and thrilled . . .

But in love? Probably not. She had said . . . And she *wouldn't* know!

So—what came next?

Well—commencement, of course. She would have walked out on that, too, but her parents were coming. And they did come. Gretchen, never letting her flag of gaiety drop, went through the ceremony, black robe and mortarboard, the tassel bit—the congratulations—the crowds of people. The University did the thing for all the schools at once in a huge tent on the main campus, with a buffet afterward . . .

And everyone, not especially her classmates, asked Gretchen where she would be interning. Her parents interspersed these greetings and congratulations with messages from home. They had hoped to bring Kathy with them, they said. "You girls have been chums for so long!"

Yes. They had been. Their parents were friends. At home, Kathy and Gretchen saw a lot of each other. They were not alike. Kathy was a dark girl with Indian-straight black hair and huge, wide eyes. She made a good foil for Gretchen's blond beauty, her love of fun—

"What is Kathy up to?" she asked her parents, her fork exploring the shrimp on her paper plate.

She only half-listened to her mother's story about why she feared Kathy was getting to be rather wild.

This was interrupted by some other character asking her where Gretchen would be interning.

Gretchen said she had other plans—and she smiled at her questioner.

"Getting married?" asked the young man.

"You're getting colder," she said airily, and walked away, as if to get some more shrimp, or whatever it was they were offering at the crowded table. She knew that she had no intern placement. Last winter, involved with the beginning of that business with Valier, she had asked for none. She had expected that she would be—

She stopped still. In front of her was a stout woman in a lavender-flowered dress. Somebody's proud mother, she supposed. But nothing for Gretchen to get so angry about.

Well, of course, the poor woman had nothing to do

with it, but Gretchen was certainly angry. Furious. For the first time she could ever remember, someone, some *human* being! had been the one to call the turn on what she would and would not do. And it was not going to happen again! No one, absolutely *no one*, was ever going to undercut her, and leave her—

She dropped her paper plate on the table; she pushed the black hat from her head and swung it by the damned tassel. She turned on her heel and went back, went fast, to where her mother was still talking to the curious, brand-new Dr. Cleveland. Dr. Koppe, equally brand-new, had joined them.

Gretchen put her arm around her mother's shoulder. "Where are you lads interning?" she asked coolly.

They told her. Cleveland was going to Chicago, and Koppe to Boston.

"And I," said Gretchen silkily, "*I* am going home."

She felt her mother jump; she saw the smile grow on her father's face.

She swallowed the anger at the back of her throat.

One of the guys—Koppe—said he understood that meant Idaho. "Don't they use medicine men out there?"

"They do," Gretchen assured him. "The air is so pure, everyone stays healthy. People live to be ninety-five without batting an eye. Why, we have one woman—" And she launched into a vivid description of Mrs. Ida B. Callier and her niece, Marcella Willis, that had even her mother laughing helplessly. And Gretchen an inch from choking on the anger which still threatened to suffocate her. She didn't want to go back to Idaho. She did not want to!

The circle about them grew. The word was repeated.

Gretchen was going back home.

"To Podunk?" asked the wife of one of the graduates. Gretchen had several times spent an evening of ham sandwiches, beans, and beer in their one-room apartment. The girl was no dummy. She, and probably others, must suspect her defeat from Valier. Otherwise she would be—

But she tossed her head and answered gayly. "I'm being brave," she told herself. "Yes, of course!" she said aloud. "I am going back to Podunk."

What were her plans there?

This drew the attention of her mother and her dad. Poor dears, this was all news to them, too. Was she going to practice? Was there a hospital?

"Oh, yes, indeed," said Gretchen blithely. "Podunk General. You've surely heard of it? We also have a shopping center. Then—the natives pick hops and fruit in season. And there's a resort hotel around every bend in the road. And you would not *believe* how those roads bend!"

The crowd grew, the laughter increased. Mr. and Mrs. Purser stood back and watched what was a sight familiar to them—their daughter attracting and delighting an audience.

They were pleased. They could save their questions until later. Now they stood happily and watched the show. These interesting young people, these fine young minds—the sunlight that came through the leaves of the tall trees, the stretches of bright lawn, the sandstone and pink granite walls of the aging buildings—it was like a painting, a brightly photographed scene, with Gretchen, their girl, as center, the gayest, the brightest of them all.

They themselves had questions to ask, but that could wait. It was enough to know that their fondest dream, their faintest hopes were to be realized. She was coming home.

"Will you open an office?" some man demanded, talking loudly to attract Gretchen's attention.

"What specialty, Gretch?" called another.

"Well, I'm going to wait to decide that," said Gretchen, serious—or pretending to be. "Until I pass my exams for licensure. If I do."

"You'll pass them," said a very tall, very thin young man. "It's all a matter of knowing the right people. And of course you *do.*"

For the briefest second, Gretchen's fury blazed in her blue eyes. "I like you, too, Butch," she said softly. "And I'll be happy to introduce you around."

This turned the laughter on the tall man, who acknowledged the sword prick with a broad, flat hand.

Gretchen watched him make his way across the grass, and she closed her eyes for a moment to fight down this terrible, this persistent rage.

She *would* go home! she told herself. She must leave this area where even a couple of people did not like her or want her around. That dislike made her uncertain, perhaps even frightened, and she did not like the experience.

She turned back to her mother, a small, pretty woman. Gretchen really loved her. "Let's get out of this," she said. "I have to move, you know, and find a place to stay until I take those exams."

"You can't get your license in Idaho?"

"I could. It's better if I do it where my school is."

"How long will that take?"

"Not too long, Mother."

"And you really don't have any plans?" asked her father. Rancher, banker, a successful man, she must be more definite with Hugh Purser, whom she both admired and loved.

"Not if I come home," she agreed. "I wasn't sure that I would do that."

"But you said . . ."

"Yes, I did. When I saw you, I knew I needed to be among the folks I love. But, meanwhile . . ."

"You'll stay and take the exams."

"Yes, and work. I have a job here. I could stay on here."

"No, Gretchen," protested her mother.

Gretchen hugged her. "Let's get out of these fancy duds, and pack my stuff," she said.

They did just that for the rest of the afternoon, moving Gretchen to the hotel. "I'll foot the bill for two weeks," said her father.

"But—"

"If you decide to stay, you can find something within your own income limits. Mine can stand the hotel for a short run."

"I think I'll stay with her," announced Mary Purser, "and not let her change her mind."

Gretchen and her father laughed, and over a late dinner Gretchen told her parents about the "job" which she had with the Federal Information Center.

"Is it medical work, dear?" asked her mother. "I suppose it would be."

"Sometimes the questions asked are medical,"

Gretchen agreed. "It's what the title says it is. An information center. We get questions of all sorts, and are supposed to be smart enough to find the answers."

"Not to know for yourself?" asked her father. He was a lean, sun-bronzed man, slow of speech, quick of mind. A black patch covered his left eye.

"Sometimes we do know," Gretchen agreed. "Where to get passports, things like that."

"It's a government office?"

"Federal Information Center."

Her father nodded. "Tell us about it."

"Well—I've worked there part time. One of the doctors was interested in it, said they could use help, and I did some off-hours' service."

"Paid for it?"

"Oh, yes."

"And you liked it."

Gretchen had liked it. The doctor she had mentioned was Erwin Valier. He probably had not been behind the offer of full-time, steady work, but if she worked there every day, she would see him, and—

She smiled brightly at her parents and told about the work done at the Center. "For instance, we had this case," she said. "I didn't do all the research. You see, this man called the Center. He was the father of a teen-aged girl who was studying abroad. He had just learned that his daughter had developed scarlet fever in Amboise, France."

"Oh, dear," said Mrs. Purser.

"Eat your lamb chops, Mary," said Hugh Purser, "and let Gretchen tell us."

"I'll do it anyway," Gretchen assured him. "Let's see.

The girl was admitted to a hospital, and the group with which she had been traveling went on to their next country and town."

"A conducted tour, dear?"

"Maybe. I think there was an American conducting a busload of students. But, anyway, the poor father wanted a report on his girl's condition."

"Of course," said Hugh Purser.

"And someone told him about our Center. He hadn't known there was such a thing."

"I wouldn't have," agreed her father.

"Well, of course, they don't exist in every city. Just in thirty-five, I think. But everyone could get the information. And get help."

"As this father did."

"Yes. He called the Center. I happened to answer the telephone. And our office head told me to call the Bureau of Consular Affairs at the Department of State."

"And did you?" asked Mary Purser, awed.

"Well, of course I did. And a cablegram was sent to the United States Embassy in France requesting that the girl's condition be checked and a report sent to the parents. This was done, and the man came in person to the Center, where he was advised about planning the girl's return home." She smiled at her parents and ate some of her dinner.

Talking about the Center, about the job she could fill there, gave her the ability to gather up the strings which Valier's blunt rejection had cut and sent floating off aimlessly. She would see him at the Center; she hoped something could be worked out between them, and if it could not, she would find a way to pay him off.

This man, no man—

He was the first man she had ever thought she loved, the first man with whom she said to herself that she had fallen in love. Perhaps all first loves happened before the woman—maybe the man, too—really knew what love was. She was old enough to know, and he certainly was old enough, experienced enough, to know what she was giving him.

But he had left her facing a blank wall. And from that hateful experience she had learned one lesson: she would never fully trust any man, never easily surrender to one, again. There must always be a good part of Gretchen Purser left to *be* Gretchen Purser!

Even if Valier, encountering her at the Center, might be ready to resume some sort of relationship—

He was not. When he came in—one evening a week—he manned the front desk, after hours, directing the operation, taking emergency questions, instigating emergency services—

When he came in the first time and found Gretchen doing some filing, he showed surprise. He said he thought she would have taken some sort of vacation. What about the licensure? Then was she going home? To get married perhaps? He knew that she had not asked for an internship.

He was polite, he was cool, but definitely the "affair" was concluded.

In return Gretchen, too, was cool and polite. She would take the exams, she said, and she had promised her parents that when she would return home.

She supposed Valier was right. A woman with an M.D. could find more rewarding service than the Center.

Though she had discovered that she liked the work, liked the place—

Three full-time employees, all women, operated the office every day, eight to four. Telephone service was available until 6 P.M. Year round, the Center received an average of nine thousand inquiries a month by phone, letter, or personal visit. In the summer, this average increased, and gave reason for Gretchen's employment. The purpose was to provide a clearinghouse for inquiries about local, state, and federal government, but it dealt with all manner of inquiries on other matters. Dr. Valier was a councilman in the suburb where he lived, which accounted for his interest. He first had looked into the sort of information given out, and then, by offering to fill in one time, became some sort of a fixture there. He arranged his professional and personal life to allow this.

He had had nothing to do with Gretchen's employment, and unless she stayed after hours, she need not see him. But she did know when he was due to come in, and she found reasons to be around on those early evenings. She might just be leaving—her bright hair freshly combed, her manner friendly, and suggesting other things she would be doing—

"I'm late," she might say. "But if I could help— You know what the calls will be. How to get National Park camping permits, how to get bugs out of a house, where does one apply for passports, and who gives the required shots."

Valier laughed. He knew what she was up to. "Did you offer to give them?"

"The shots? Not me. But you call yourself *doctor*, so watch out, sir. Watch out!"

"My specialty is crank calls," he reminded her.

"Sure, sure. Imagine their putting the listing in the Yellow Pages as NEED MORE HELP? and then listing our number. I wish we'd kept count on all the bright ones who are inspired to call and say, 'I'll be right over to help you!' "

Dr. Valier nodded, and Gretchen left.

Two weeks later, he himself came in early, and was ready to laugh with her over the request from a pregnant woman for Hungarian names for her child. "What will you do?" he asked Gretchen.

"Find some Hungarian names," she assured him. "The GSO would never forgive me if I didn't."

"I suppose not, but—"

"I thought I'd try the universities and the public library."

"Fine!" he agreed. "That's smart thinking, Gretchen."

"I have my moments."

His duties required him only to take telephone calls, listing the problems in such detail that the regular employees could handle them. During the summer these extra people took care of handling the sale of consumer products information for pamphlets which would answer questions on automobiles, financing, child care, food, housing and fabrics.

Gretchen had done this work and knew that it could be boring. She thought he might welcome a diversion or two. So when, in the course of her regular work, she acted on a telephone question left by Dr. Valier, she felt justified in telling him the outcome of that interesting inquiry, and the round-the-world search which she had made.

The doctor had left a note, complete with name, address, telephone number. Someone had found a cat. This indicated that someone had lost a cat. A Siamese cat. It carried a vaccination tag, with a number, and the address: NAVAL STATION, P.R.

Gretchen, finding the inquiry and Dr. Valier's familiar initials on her desk the next day, went to work.

She was successful, and on his next evening of duty, she stayed at the office to announce to him triumphantly that she had found his cat.

She was looking her prettiest in a brown linen dress, slim brown slippers, and a necklace of carved wooden beads, as well as her friendliest smile. "We found your cat," she told him.

His face was blank. "What cat?"

"The one that was lost. Remember? NAVAL STATION, P.R."

"Oh, yes. That cat!"

"That cat, indeed. Well, we located the owner."

He paused to answer the telephone. "Tell me," he said then.

"Oh, we—I—called the recruiting office. They said P.R. meant Puerto Rico."

"That sounds reasonable."

She laughed. "Yes, it does, doesn't it? So—next I called the San Juan Base veterinarian; he checked his files, said the cat belonged to a discharged service man. And guess what? He lives only two doors from the woman who found the cat!"

Dr. Valier rubbed his hand down his face. "And the cat probably wasn't lost at all."

She considered this. "His family was glad to have him back . . ."

"No doubt. Gretchen?"

"Yes."

"Do you like the work you do here?"

"Yes. Yes, I do. I'm surprised at how much I like it."

"But you have taken your exams?"

"Yes, Doctor, I have."

"And you should have passed them. So I suppose—I hope—you are going home."

"I thought I might try to intern."

"In one of our hospitals?"

"Yes."

He shook his head. "It isn't a good idea, Gretchen."

"I'd do the work."

"I'm sure you would. Just as you do the work here. But it won't get you what you think you want, my dear. I'm sorry, but it won't."

That evening, she offered no further argument, but she kept it in her plans to manage some way with Erwin Valier to leave the city, and him, with a few points in her favor. She no longer cared about *him*, but she must leave her mark, somehow.

When word came that she had passed her licensure exams, she gave some time to a debate with herself, and afterward she knew that she had made the wrong decision. She should have left for home without seeing Valier again. Then he might wonder what had happened to her. He might.

She could have worked into a full-time job at the Center, or she could try for the internship. Either move might anger Valier, but at least he would see her, he would think about her.

When she had decided what to do, she went to see him at the hospital, the busy doctor, brisk and handsome in his white coat. And she . . .

He was surprised to see her. "Gretchen?" he asked.

She smiled. "I told you I might apply for intern service. I thought you would give me an indorsement."

Instantly he was angry. His lips thinned, his jaw set.

She would never forgive herself for crying. Humiliated, frustrated—the man actually was *kind* to her!

She packed and returned to Idaho, carrying with her this one complete failure—the first failure she had ever known along the line of her personal popularity. Angry in a way she had never before known, she left the city, hourly hardening her resolve to be herself, to be the Gretchen she knew herself to be—admired, and popular, especially by and with herself. And never, never, *never* would she again think of Dr. Valier!

CHAPTER 2

As HAD always happened before, the plane trip home was a triumph. From the skycap who checked her bags in at the city airport to the pilot who came out to speak to the passengers, Gretchen's bruised and wounded vanity was soothed and restored. Eyes followed her admiringly when she went along the concourse at Denver, head up, her stride confident. Eyes brightened all along the aisle when she entered the plane and selected a seat beside a white-haired woman absorbed in the book in her hands.

The stewardess on that flight knew her; several passengers did. She welcomed them as she welcomed the mountains and the salt-edged great lake below them, gratefully satisfied. At Salt Lake City, a dozen of the boarding passengers knew her; they asked where she had been. Was she going to stick around? Was there any truth to the nasty rumor that she was now a doctor? "Just tell me where to go when I'm sick," said one man loudly. "I know who I want to take my pulse!"

It was corny, and fun, and ego-building. Gretchen

could deplane with her head up and her smile genuinely happy. Her father's attorney was on the plane, and he escorted her from it in a lordly manner, beaming at those who waited at the end of the passageway. He was a portly man, and dressed in a somewhat exaggerated manner—broad-brimmed white hat, string tie, and kid-glove-soft Western boots. Gretchen had known him all her life. There was one man she could trust!

"Thank you, Judge," she said warmly when he handed her over to her beaming parents and her eager, smiling friends.

"Best trip I ever made!" declared Judge Warrington.

"What you doin', ridin' with that pretty girl, Judge?" some man called from the crowd.

"Don't tell him," said Gretchen fliply, and the whole airport shook with laughter.

"How are you, Dad?" said Gretchen. "Mother?"

"Glad to have you home," said her father proudly.

"You look wonderful, dear," said her mother.

Then Kathy Bennett took over, springing at Gretchen, her dark hair flying. "Oh, it's so *good* to have you back, Gretch!" she cried. "Mr. Purser, don't you ever give her plane fare *again!*"

It was great fun, the laughter, all the people, known and unknown, and all smiling at the tall, handsome girl in her red linen suit, so happy, one could tell, to be home again.

It was great, Gretchen said, to go into the house again, to see and to touch all the familiar things. Yes, she had eaten dinner—

"Corned beef sandwiches," said Kathy scornfully.

Gretchen smiled at her. "It was good corned beef," she

pointed out. She smoothed the new covers on the two couches that flanked the deep fireplace, and said, yes, she would love some ice cream.

This was a ritual for anyone coming in on the evening plane. Ice cream served in bowls, with chocolate sauce or crème de menthe offered, cake on a tray . . . and talk.

That night, often, three people were talking at once, and many questions went unanswered. But Hugh and Mary Purser could beam at their daughter, and Kathy could sit beside her, bubbling with news about their friends. There would be some parties, she told Gretchen. "We're all so glad to have you home."

When she left, Gretchen walked down the street with Kathy, relishing the thin, cool air, the moonlight and the stars that blazed so close overhead. "I can't figure why I ever left this place," she said.

"To learn to be a famous doctor," Kathy assured her.

Gretchen sniffed.

"Are you going to practice, Gretch?" asked her friend.

"Oh, I don't know what I'm going to do, Kathy," said Gretchen. "Sleep a lot for one thing, go to those parties you talked about—" She looked out across the valley. "What more could a girl want?"

"It suits me," said Kathy contentedly. "See you tomorrow, honey."

Gretchen walked home, relishing the fact that anyone could walk safely along a residential street at almost midnight. She smiled fondly at the picture her home made in the moonlight. A Norman-style stone house, complete with a square tower, and floor-to-ceiling windows, it had been built nearly a hundred years before, a mansion surrounded by acres and acres of ground. Now it still had wide lawns, and many flower beds; the carriage house had become a garage, and the family no longer kept a cow, or even a pony for their little girl.

Inside were high ceilings, modern plumbing and heating; the rooms were huge. Gretchen's bedroom was as big as the commons room at the student dormitory where she had lived while getting her M.D. It was a formal, somewhat dark room, but she loved every inch of it. The half-poster bed, the crewel upholstery of the wing chair and the window draperies, the rich Oriental on the floor, bordered with the wide-planked floor, rich with decades of waxing and polishing.

She found pajamas, bathed and fell into bed. Tomorrow she would unpack and think up some answers for all the questions she would be asked.

The next day she found that her mother had arranged a luncheon for her friends—a dozen young women, half of them married and with families, some of the others working, one teaching at an Indian school, one with her own boutique.

On Friday night, "everyone" always went to the dinner at the country club. There tables of friends vied with other groups for noise and gaiety. There was dancing, and a busy bar, and a doctor or two who made a point of asking Gretchen where she was going to work.

"My M.D. is so brand-new," she answered, "and I haven't interned."

"We can use you," said each man.

This gave Gretchen a little to think about, but not much. She was not ready to make any commitments. One doctor—Biron Wagner—she knew quite well. He was Chief of Staff at the town's large hospital, a government-backed institution. She should be flattered by his interest in her.

The other man—Gretchen was charming to him, but mentally she classed him as an "old fool." He had been in private practice since long before she could remember. But that night she let him talk to her about his "study" of acupuncture, his use of it, his belief in it. She confessed that, beyond attending a couple of lectures and demonstrations by visiting physicians from Mainland China, she knew little about the technique. Oh, no, she would not let him use his pins on her!

Kathy rescued her from Dr. Fielder—and Gretchen decided that the young woman was indeed drinking too much. Halfway through the evening, she was wobbling. She had brought up a tall, bright-eyed man in a plaid coat who was, said Kathy, Til Holt, the City Manager, and anxious to meet Gretchen.

He was tall, lean, with weathered skin and keen blue eyes. His hair was a light red. Gretchen smiled at him, and talked to him. Holt was quite a man, she decided, and definitely sexy.

"He's a bachelor," had said Kathy when introducing him, "and he says he means to stay that way."

"That should make life safer for the ladies," drawled Gretchen. She danced with Holt, she went out with him to look at the moon, and she said that she was glad he had come to Idaho.

He, like everyone else, asked her what she planned to do.

And to each one she replied, "Tomorrow I've promised to ride the line with Dad."

She did ride with her father, going up into the hills,

towing the metal trailer that was like an enormous bullet shining behind them. They stayed over Sunday, and Gretchen confessed to being saddle tender. But she loved every minute up in the "hills"—the rough, friendly talk of the hands, the sun hot, the nights cold. The pines . . . "Oh, the pines!" she cried in ecstasy. And the swift, green rivers, with their water as clear and as delicious as the air.

She came home replete, content, not even feeling her aching limbs or the blister she had acquired cooking bacon and eggs for her father. That tall, lean man was happy, too. Gretchen gazed at him fondly when they drove home on Monday morning. He was thin, and as brown as leather. His black eye patch would distinguish him anywhere. She knew that he could change from flannel shirt and cord breeches to English-tailored gray flannel and look the part in each one.

"What are you going to do, sugar?" he asked mildly, as they dropped down and down again toward the valley, and home.

"Do I have to decide right away, Boss?" she asked.

"Not so far as I'm concerned. You'll be happier when you do."

"I could decide wrong."

"Why should you be different? We all have to explore life, and select the place to build our nests."

She said nothing.

"The doctors' society is holding a dinner and reception for you on Thursday night."

"Mother told me. Are you going?"

"Oh, yes. We're your family."

On Tuesday morning Gretchen cleaned the trailer, a

fixed rule for all who went camping. That afternoon she went to the beauty parlor. On Wednesday she consented to go with her mother to buy some clothes and pay a call on the widow of Judge Warrington who had died, unexpectedly, the day after Gretchen's return home. Gretchen deplored both excursions.

"I don't need clothes," she told her mother.

"A pretty dress helps you to have a good time, dear."

So the pretty dress was bought, the call of condolence made, and Gretchen had no strength left to object when her mother decided that they might as well call on Mrs. Callier, too, and her niece. They lived even closer to the Pursers than did Kathy. Ida B. was ninety-six, her niece was about seventy, a large, stout woman.

"As dull as ditch water!" declared Gretchen.

"Isn't the term dishwater, dear?" asked her mother.

"It could be. Marcella qualifies for both. Oh, Mother, don't make me go there again."

"All right, dear. But when you are ninety-six—"

Gretchen turned swiftly. "Me?" she cried, unbelieving.

Her mother laughed. "I can't imagine it, either."

"Does she actually melt down all the leftovers in the candy she gets as gifts at Christmas and Valentine's, then cut it into squares and *expect* us to eat it?"

"She thinks it is clever, dear."

"You ate a piece!"

"Yes, I did. It pleased her."

"That's where you make your mistake, to try to please her. She takes advantage of you."

Her mother smiled patiently. "She's a wonderful old lady."

"Born to be hanged," muttered Gretchen, taking the boxes and bags upstairs.

For the next day or two she filled her time with the little pleasant things that meant home. She went on errands for her mother, she visited with her friends, going to see their homes and their babies, buying a wedding gift at the boutique. "I think I'd like having some sort of shop," she told the owner.

"Oh, Gretchen, you couldn't do anything but doctor, could you? Your father would be so disappointed."

"Yes, he would." And Gretchen would be, too, really. She missed the work and the busy atmosphere of the hospital. "I'll see," she told the boutique owner.

On Thursday evening she dressed carefully in the gown her mother had urged her to buy—a red dress, silky. Unadorned. Her hair shone, her smile was happy, she talked eagerly and happily to the assembled doctors. From what she heard, five staff doctors from the hospital were present. She was seated beside Dr. Wagner, a spray of white flowers pinned on her shoulder. Of course old Dr. Fielder was there.

"Is he on your staff?" asked Gretchen. The man was old, his hair rose in white tufts on his otherwise bald head, his eyes were rheumy, his lips trembled, and his hands. He talked endlessly . . .

"We let him come around," said Dr. Wagner. "He doesn't want to admit that age has touched him. But when it comes to caring for the sick, Gretchen . . ."

She nodded. "It takes so many acuities," she agreed. "Brain, eye, hand . . ."

"You belong on our staff, my dear," said Dr. Wagner. "Your medical school record is excellent."

Her eyes flared wide. "You checked?"

"Of course. We need you."

She turned to the food before her. "Which are your other staff members?" she asked politely.

"Well, we don't have too large a house staff. Seven with me and Fielder. But of course there are a dozen or more visitings, men who have offices in the towns around here, who bring in patients, and are permitted to attend."

"I see. I suppose I've met them?"

"They evidently made small impression."

"That isn't it. I've been away for four—really eight years. So I'm new, and to be faced with fifteen or twenty doctors, all of them with strange names . . . I'll sort them out later."

"Of course you will. Now, I'll point out the house staff. There's Tipton over there beside the blond lady in blue."

"Internist," said Gretchen.

"That's right. A good man. Down the table from him, the dark man with the beard is Shaw. D.O."

Gretchen turned sharply. "Really?"

"The state licenses osteopaths. This hospital was built . . ."

"I know. With government money. How do you work with them?"

"Quite well, at times. Patiently, at others. My chief quarrel with them is their passion for publicity. M.D.'s have never . . . The other one on the house staff is Giamonco, internist and part-time radiologist." Hc pointed this man out.

"Good?"

"Adequate."

He identified the other doctors, and Gretchen paid close attention. Halfway through the discussion, she wondered who would be the "Valier" of the group. Tilford Holt, perhaps, who was not a doctor, but who had brought Kathy to the dinner, and together they seemed to be having a ball.

By the dinner's end, the best promise Gretchen gave to Dr. Wagner was that she would come to the hospital and look around. "I don't suppose I should give up medicine," she conceded.

"Certainly not. You should establish your license here—there would be no difficulty—and you should help me."

"I'll come to see you," she promised.

There were no speeches, no program at that dinner. Some of the guests began to dance to the small orchestra. Gretchen danced. With Til Holt, debating with herself if she should flirt with the man as Kathy did. And prove he was another Valier? She would know how to handle him if he were. Now he seemed only charming, and interesting. She danced with her father, and to her amusement, the short, dark-bearded D.O.—Shaw—cut in. He was, she discovered, rather pompous, insisting on professional talk.

Gretchen was as charming to him as she had been to Holt, but she enjoyed it much less. She rather liked the City Manager, and it was he, a half hour later, who said he thought it was time for "this girl" to answer the question she had been evading for a week, and tell the world what it was she planned to do. She couldn't leave the city—he'd had all roads closed to her—but what *were* her plans?

Gretchen shook her hair back from her face, she looked around at the people who awaited her answer. At least thirty of her friends, leaning forward, eyes eager—

"Close your mouths," she bade them. "I'll tell you. I came home—really I did—to get married."

This was a stunning announcement. Breaths were drawn in, then an instant clamor arose. People in the next room heard the word repeated, and repeated again. Even her father came to the wide doorway and looked at her in concern. She had not told them . . .

"Who?" everyone asked. "Who, Gretchen?"

She fingered the little rhinestone buttons on the front of her red chiffon shirtwaist dress. "You sound like a tree full of owls," she told those close to her.

"But *who* are you going to marry?" demanded Kathy, pushing her way forward. "What's his name? Do we know him?"

Gretchen shrugged. "You may know him. I don't. I don't know his name."

"But you said . . ."

"That I'd picked out my career. I have. I am going to be married."

"You can still doctor," said Dr. Tipton.

Gretchen glanced his way. She was having a wonderful time. "Yes, I can," she agreed.

"Are you going to?"

"Probably." This created a buzz of talk. But there still was the matter . . .

"She's up for grabs, maybe," said one man's voice loudly.

Gretchen laughed. "I always have been, George," she challenged the speaker, who found the laughter turned on him.

But there were those who still insisted that she must have a man in mind . . .

She tried to say that she did not.

Some other joker said that all eligible men should go to one end of the room.

"We don't need to," drawled Til Holt. "She's looked us over, and she still can't call a name."

Gretchen smiled. She did like that man, she decided. Did he belong to Kathy? She could find out . . .

The discussion turned into a noisy riot, and finally, with thirty or more people still there to hear what she said, she declared that she had decided to marry the first man who asked her for a date.

Now the hubbub was really tremendous. There was laughter, squealing laughter, roars from the men—a pretended stampede—a pretense of terror—"Let me out of here," cried someone. "I get these impulses . . ."

Kathy Bennett, more than a little tiddly, asked everyone to *imagine* being married to *Gretchen!*

In the pause that followed, Susan Warrington's low voice was heard to say, "She'd be a great catch."

Gretchen heard her. She turned away. "Let's all go home," she said, sounding tired. Susan, widowed a week, should not have come to this party. Gretchen should not have . . .

No one had believed a foolish word, of course. She assured her parents of this; she assured herself.

To still her mother's anxiety, she told that she had promised to go to the hospital on Monday.

"Will you work there, dear?"

"Biron Wagner thinks I will, and he's almost never wrong."

She hoped this satisfied her father, too, but when she found herself in her bedroom, and almost ready for bed, she wasn't sure. Of that, or of anything. She had played the fool; she acknowledged that. But something had set her off—her speculation about Til Holt, her linking that truly delightful man with Valier—Should Gretchen warn Kathy about such men?

She laughed shortly, and turned off the light. As if she could tell Kathy anything about men!

It was Gretchen who needed instruction, who had needed it last spring.

Valier, and his hold on her . . . Right now, just to remember him brought such cold fury that she could feel her limbs tremble. Never having surrendered before, and never rejected, never swamped and smothered with frustration, it was the first real defeat she had ever known, and it continued to fill her with cold fury. That there should exist one person beside herself who knew of that defeat . . .

She had left Valier and any chance that he could watch her. But tonight he was there behind the things she had said— Oh, she did wish she had not made such a fool of herself!

She thought back over every word; she remembered what others had said, their faces—their amused disbelief that she could be serious. And there was her out.

Another thing: to reassure her parents, she had told of her promise to go to the hospital on Monday. From that visit she probably would get to work, and the work probably would be good. In a short time, people would forget the silly promise; she would forget it.

Starting *now!*

She thumped her pillows, looked at the waning moon outside her window, and thought about the hospital and Biron Wagner. What would he ask her to do? He had said something about emergency room work being a good place to start. Was their hospital qualified for intern training? Even if it was not, Dr. Wagner could give her that training—the responsibilities, the instruction and the actual experience. Yes, that could work out very well.

And she could say that she had no time for dates or weddings. Maybe she would say nothing, maybe just meet any inquiries with a blank stare. Since childhood that procedure had got her out of scrapes.

She fell asleep.

But the next day, Kathy Bennett was into the house before noon to talk over the party of the night before. And blank stares, talk of interning under Dr. Wagner, would not serve to divert her from a discussion of the announcement which Gretchen had made.

Gretchen tried. She even asked Kathy if there was a *thing* between her and Til Holt.

"One-sided still," said Kathy readily. "I'd fasten to that man, but he's as slick as a trout. And no girl yet has found bait or lure to snag him, including me."

"He asked me last night if I thought you were serious in what you'd said—I suppose he was planning to ask you for a date. I told him that I was sure you had been." She faced Gretchen, her dark eyes round. "Were you?" she asked.

Gretchen knew that she was becoming angry again. "Yes," she said coolly. "I think it's as good a way as any to select the man. You might tell your City Manager."

"Or warn him," said Kathy. "I won't have to say you are crazy. He'll decide that for himself."

"I've done crazy things before."

"But, Gretchen—"

"Everybody expects me to get married. You expected me to when we finished college. But I went off to medical school."

"And I thought you were crazy. Yes, I did." Kathy was smiling.

"And you're still expecting me to get married."

"Well—sometime, yes."

"*Everybody* expects me to get married," said Gretchen again. "Right?"

"Yes, I suppose they do. You're popular with the men, you'd be a great catch, like Susan Warrington said last night."

"Mhmmmmn. So I'll marry the first guy who asks me for a date, and settle the whole thing."

"Even if . . . ?" asked Kathy, awed, but eager, too.

"Even if it's the grocery boy."

"The grocery boy wouldn't— Besides, there aren't any grocery boys these days."

"They have them at the supermarket, the sack boys. I get along fine with *them!*"

"You are crazy," said Kathy.

Gretchen thought she could put the whole happening out of her mind. And to some extent she did. She went to the hospital, she agreed to work there six hours a day, five days a week, half-promising to extend the hours and her services, "When I become of some use to you, Doctor."

"I'll make use of you," Dr. Wagner promised.

As she had expected, she liked the work she did; she liked having regular hours and duties. She began to speak of herself as Dr. Purser, and many so spoke of her. She hoped, she hoped, she *hoped* people would stop wondering if she really would get married. If she really would . . .

And then Ida B. Callier got into the picture and thrust a few sticks into the smoothly turning wheels.

One afternoon, Gretchen came back from the hospital —she had been working from eight until two, but sometimes stayed longer. Her mother had left a note for her to call Marcella Willis, who was Mrs. Callier's niece.

Gretchen disliked the old lady, and considered her a nuisance. She thoroughly despised Marcella. The woman was a crashing bore, her physical presence offended Gretchen's sense of what a woman should do with her body. Marcella was big, and she was fat. Rather than display her white, uncurled hair, she wore turbans. Old turbans around home, new, bright turbans in public. "Africa learned from her," Gretchen once had said, and was quoted. The town praised Marcella for coming to live with her aunt. Gretchen thought it was more a matter of feathering Marcella's own nest. Though she really did not care. She tossed her mother's note into the wastebasket. If Mrs. Callier was giving one of her parties, Gretchen did not mean to attend. The old lady made what she called daiquiris by saving the juice from various cans of fruit, adding whiskey and lemonade, cooling the mess with ice cubes . . .

No, sir! Not a Callier party!

She went up to her room, showered, put on slacks and a thin wool top, and came down to the small fire in the family room. This day had turned a little chilly, a promise that summer was about over. The little Chinese maid told her where her mother was. Working at something the girl called a free market. Gretchen smiled at her. She had meant flea market, of course.

She was half asleep in her deep chair when Mrs. Purser returned, looking very tired. Gretchen jumped to her feet, and insisted that her mother sit down. "*Wow!*" she breathed. "You've been through the mill!"

"These things are moneymakers," sighed Mary Purser. "But they are hard on my back."

"And your feet, and your hands—just look at them! Look, my darling, you are going to take a hot bath and go to bed. Dinner will be served there! Did you eat lunch?"

Her mother said, "Oh, yes," but Gretchen didn't believe her. And she couldn't have dinner in bed. It would frighten Hugh just terribly. But she would take the bath. Had Gretchen called Marcella?

"No," said Gretchen, urging her mother up the stairs.

"But, darling . . ."

"A hot bath, sweetheart."

"Yes, I'll take one. And change my clothes."

"With the bath in between."

Mary giggled. "Of course. But, Gretchen, I think Ida B. is sick."

"I wouldn't be surprised, living with Marcella."

"They do quarrel. Did you know that? Everybody thinks it's a beautiful relationship, but I happen to know they quarrel."

"Mhmmnn," said Gretchen, going into the bathroom to turn on the water. She knew that Mary had followed her to the door.

"Do go down there, darling," said her mother.

Gretchen poured bath oil into the bubbling water. It smelled of roses.

"Marcella called you 'doctor,'" said Mrs. Purser, laughing a little. "She said that Auntie wanted Dr. Purser to come down."

Gretchen straightened. "Look, Mother . . ."

"Please do, darling. It wouldn't hurt you."

Gretchen, in her pale blue slacks and pullover, towered above her mother. "You'll take your bath, and lie down for at least an hour?"

"Yes, I promise."

"All right, then. But not because Marcella called me 'doctor.' I'm going to tell her never to do it again."

Her mother smiled uncertainly, and Gretchen departed. "It would please everybody," she grumbled, "if I'd take my little black bag." She had such a bag, packed away with her books and stuff from medical school. Every graduating student was given such a bag by one of the pharmaceutical companies. Gretchen had considered throwing the thing away. She could not picture herself ever carrying one.

She ran down the stairs, she ran down the driveway, went around the hedge, and down the slope of the street, tall and slender, her hair rising and falling against her shoulders. It was dark-gold hair, and at times, in the sun, it shone almost pure gold, bright and rich. It was thick, with a smooth curl away from her face and throat. Her skin was white, though clear red shone through against her high cheekbones. Hers was the kind of fair skin that didn't burn or mottle. Gretchen was a beautiful young woman, and she was well aware of the fact. Being aware, she put the fact out of her thoughts.

This late afternoon, with the sun streaking red between mauve and gray clouds in the western sky, she went to the front door of the Callier house. A pale lavender front door, of all things! She touched the bell and looked around, thinking of her mother and the flea market. Why hadn't Marcella worked at that? Gretchen decided that she would ask her.

The interior of the Callier house was dark; no window shades or drapery was ever opened there. It was warm, and smelled mustily of stale air, thick rug padding under the Oriental rugs, of ancient upholstery.

Marcella greeted Gretchen. "I'm so glad you came, Doctor," was her first attempt.

"The name is Gretchen, as it has been for the twenty-five years I've known you, Miss Marcella." And she brushed past the big woman.

"Mother said"—she spoke over her shoulder—"that Mrs. Callier was ill."

"She thinks she is," said Marcella wryly.

Gretchen glanced back at her. "I don't do private practice."

"We both thought you would make an exception."

She would not, Gretchen promised herself. But she went on to the old lady's sitting room. She had been familiar with this home since childhood. Red walls, red carpet, the room was crowded with furniture, its bookshelves contained all manner of knickknacks—plastic flowers in ornate arrangements were set about—and Ida B. sat swathed in shawls, sunken into a deep, overstuffed chair. She had, years before, broken her hip, and a walker stood beside the chair. She had had cataract surgery, and today she wore a green eyeshade against the light of the lamp at the other side of her chair. She tipped this at a rakish angle so that she could peer up at Gretchen.

"I called this morning," she greeted the young woman.

"I am at the hospital all day."

"I heard, but I thought Mary would call and tell you that I needed you."

Gretchen pushed a half-dozen pillows out of the way and sat down on the couch. "Mother left a note. She was working at the flea market today. I suppose Miss Marcella did, too."

"Oh, she's not able. You know she has this terrible arthritis."

"Does she?" asked Gretchen. She didn't care, one way or the other.

"Oh, yes! She can't even get out of bed before nine-thirty or ten every morning, and she must nap for two hours after lunch."

Gretchen said nothing.

"Maybe you learned something new to do for her," suggested Ida B.

"Mother asked me to come down here to see you, Mrs. Callier."

The old lady sighed. "I get dizzy spells."

She was ninety-six. Of course she got dizzy spells.

"Who's your doctor?" Gretchen asked.

"It's been Dr. Tipton, but all he says is that I need fresh air and different food."

"He's a good doctor."

"Aren't *you* a good one?" She attempted what was meant to be an arch smile.

Gretchen shrugged. "I don't know."

"I believe you will be, and besides, you've been my girl since I sold you your first formal."

This was a fiction which Gretchen and her mother tried to ignore. Gretchen's first "formal," a matter of flower-sprigged dimity and a rose ribbon sash, had been bought at a shop in Salt Lake City for a recital given by the students of the local music academy. Gretchen was twelve at the time.

Mrs. Callier was going on and on. "You wanted a black dress and your mother didn't want you to have black, but I told her all the girls had them, and she finally gave in. Oh, Gretchen, I do miss my store! If it weren't for Marcella, I'd open one again."

At her age? Gretchen laughed.

"I could!" declared the old lady.

"Not if you're really sick."

"I have these dizzy spells. That's why I called you. You're a doctor now, and just starting out. I thought I should . . ."

Gretchen stared at her. Had she really thought . . . ? "Well, thank you very much!" she said crisply. "But I don't have an office practice, you know."

"What do you do?"

"I'm working at the hospital where needed. In the

emergency service, though today I gave physicals to a batch of candy stripers."

"Oh, you'll get patients of your own, dear. It's hard, starting out. And you grew up here, so people still think of you as a child."

"I suppose," said Gretchen indifferently. Though she had met with that attitude a time or two in the emergency room. She stood up.

"Aren't you even going to listen to my heart, Gretchen? I have a bad heart, you know."

Gretchen laughed. "And you've lived to be ninety-six?"

"Well, I take care of myself. Though I've had some terrible illnesses. Pneumonia, and my hip—and my heart stopped completely one time. And then there was the time when Mr. Callier and I went to the World's Fair in nineteen fifteen, and I got sick in Seattle, and they did thirteen operations on me."

Gretchen stared at her. The statistics were making her head swim. Sixty-five years ago this shrunken old lady had had—

"Thirteen what kind of operations?" she asked sternly.

"Oh, I can't remember them all. It's on my record in Dr. Tipton's office. Or you could ask Dr. Fielder. He was my doctor here, then."

That figured. And Gretchen would ask him. Out of pure curiosity.

She managed her departure, and at the door she told Marcella to follow Dr. Tipton's advice. "Take her outside, or open some windows in here," she said.

"Auntie would die. These windows haven't been opened in forty years!"

Gretchen shook her head. "Do you have someone to help with her, to bathe her—things like that?"

"She takes her own bath."

"She couldn't get in or out of a tub. Or, do you have a shower?"

"No. She takes sponge baths."

Gretchen stared at the big woman. She could help the old lady if she wanted to. "I don't think she could possibly clean herself that way," she said harshly.

"She thinks she does. She has no body odor like some folks."

"Why not?"

Miss Willis shrugged. "That's what she claims."

Gretchen opened the lavender door. "I'd get some fresh air in the house," she said, "and let some of this forty-year stuff out."

She didn't know why she was so angry. She surely had a half hour to give to an old lady. But—she was angry. She hoped none of her other friends would try to help her get started. She would tell her parents and the servants . . .

"Oh, forget it!" she said aloud. "Handle things yourself."

CHAPTER 3

But Gretchen was curious enough, the next day, to look up Mrs. Callier's record. Sure enough, there was the sixty-year-old report. A hysterectomy, with appendix removed and a small cyst below the left breast, benign . . . "And two ovaries, and two tubes . . ." muttered Gretchen, glassy-eyed. It might not add up to thirteen items, but some hyperbole was understandable.

"In some circles, it would make a funny story," she decided. But she definitely would not make any more house calls.

Her mother had asked her what was wrong with Ida B.

"Nothing that a good turning out wouldn't help," said Gretchen. "Mother, that house is so musty— Did you ever hear of anybody not having any body odor?"

Mrs. Purser shook her head. "I don't believe the subject was ever discussed, dear."

Gretchen hugged her. "I'm sure it wasn't."

"Are you going to the party up at Snowline, dear?"

"Oh, sure." Gretchen went to the window and gazed

out at the folds of bare brown hills, up to the distant peaks that already were frosted with snow. The *party* was going to be an expedition up to the lodge at the beginning of primitive country, then a trek on horseback up and up, to camp overnight, and then descend . . .

"Who's giving the party, dear?"

"Nobody's *giving* it, Mother. A bunch of us will take our own gear, pay our own way. Kathy told me about it, and suggested that I'd like to go, so I'm going."

"Did you get supplies? Have you clothes?"

"I have everything. Food, sleeping bag—the works."

"Are you driving your car?" The one her father had found "sitting in the garage" when she came home.

"No. I'm riding with Tilford Holt and Kathy. Probably someone else. That twenty miles of logging road takes a man's hand."

Til had not asked her. There was a thing going on between her and Til Holt, whom she continued to like.

Weary of the jokes made to her and about her because of her fool declaration at the medical society dinner—the situation even interfered with the work she was doing at the hospital, and which she rather enjoyed—she and Til had built up a running gag, which they both did enjoy, though Gretchen believed she played it more intensely than did the attractive City Manager.

From the first introduction to him, Gretchen had been intrigued by the man's indomitable bachelorhood. Something, someone, she told herself, should show him that he, too, could be had.

He detected her position, and teased her about it.

"Kathy Bennett would be glad to help," she challenged him.

"I'm sure. There also are others."

"I'm sure of that! Why, man, you must not be able to sleep at nights, guarding your defenses."

It was fun, such sparring.

She and Holt genuinely liked each other. They made good company for the whole crowd with which their group "ran." If she could ever get the man to ask her for a date—even for a cup of coffee when he'd come to the hospital and encounter her— But he was cagey. He, too, remembered her declaration, and respected her ability to make good on it.

"I'll marry the first man who asks me for a date," she had said. And not meant it. Though now . . . She wished he would ask her for that date, and she could then know what would happen next.

Til knew she wanted him to ask her, and he chose to make a delightful game of not quite doing it.

"Are you coming with us up to Primitive?" he asked her, speaking of the expedition into the mountains.

"Aren't you going to ask me?" she would challenge him when he talked about a party at the country club.

"No need," he had answered that time, and airily. "I know your father is a stockholder as well as a member."

Meeting her in the hospital coffee shop, he would call to her. "I'm having some coffee," he said. "And I'll pay for a second cup that shouldn't go to waste."

Gretchen laughed and sat down beside him. "I feel sorry for the woman who finally hobbles you," she said.

"So do I," he agreed. "My kind nature is what keeps her out of the picture."

It was a challenge, but she made no more promises, even to herself. She was going to watch her words, and her step, from now on.

As they started the trip to Primitive, with the white peak of Grand Pré drawing ever closer, the pine forests dark and fragrant about them, snow caught into the rock crevices as the road mounted. Gretchen debated asking Til to help get her out of the predicament in which she found herself. They need not go all the way to a wedding —but if he would give her an invitation, and she would announce his capture—perhaps in the presence of their friends—the gag would be fun, and the broken engagement laid to Gretchen's whim. She had the reputation of not wanting a thing once she possessed it. And the silly proclamation could be forgotten! Would Til go along with such a scheme? He might. She thought she would ask him.

The three cars, carrying a dozen young people, swept up and around the hills, skirted the deep canyons, pressed against the towering walls of shining black rock, swept out across one of the valley open spaces where flowers still bloomed and deer watched them curiously from the roadside. They met logging trucks; they followed their trail along narrow roads.

About noon they reached the last lodge, the last building on the road. They would eat lunch, fasten their gear to pack ponies, with some carrying their bedrolls behind their saddles. Gretchen did. Her father had taught her to be a good trail rider and camper.

She had thought she knew who were in the party until they all sat together along the pine table for their lunch. Then Til brought up a man whom she had never seen before. She was surprised and did not immediately understand that he was in their group.

"Have you been camping?" she asked. "How are things uptrail? Did you see any bears?"

Til bent over to cover her mouth with his hand. "She talks too much," he told the stranger. "Gretch, this is Clancy Cobbins. He's lately come to town, and joined the Warrington law firm."

Yes, her father had said that the established firm had brought in someone to help take care of the legal load. Judge Warrington's sudden death had made this necessary.

"I expected someone paunchy," she said now.

Til laughed. "Good old Gretchen, *never* knows when to keep her mouth shut."

The new man was watching her with alert brown eyes. He was attractive. Even in flannel shirt and jeans he had a crisp elegance. Well!

"Clancy?" she asked, turning her shoulder on Til Holt.

"Corruption of Clarence."

"Oh, my." She laughed. "Parents do awful things to their children, don't they?"

"Yes, they do. Mine gave me the nickname. It's got me through." He had a great speaking voice, deep and vibrant.

Gretchen pushed down along the bench. "Won't you sit down?" she asked. She looked around the room. "Did Susan come?" she asked.

"Susan?"

Gretchen glanced up at Til, who stood watching her, a spark in his hazel eyes. "Mrs. Warrington," he explained to the Cobbins chap.

"Oh, no, she didn't come," he said. "Is she a mountain climber, too?"

"We all have to be, to some extent. But this is to be a trail ride, not—"

"You'll go up, won't you?"

"Oh, yes," laughed Gretchen. "We certainly shall go up. Til, shouldn't you be eating?"

"This looks like more fun," he said.

"Go eat!" she instructed him. "We want to get going."

He put his hand on the new man's shoulder. "Be careful," he said solemnly. "Our Gretchen is a maneater."

The new man laughed. "I suspect it's a pleasure," he declared.

"Well, don't ever say I didn't warn you." He went down to the end of the table where Kathy sat.

Clancy was a fine addition to their crowd. He was amused by what Til Holt had said. He answered Gretchen's questions—where he was living. At a hotel. Where he had come from. Denver.

"Oh, then you know mountains."

"Not like these. Holt has promised to take me hunting."

"Watch it. You know the hills around our city?"

"Yes. Beautiful."

"You can walk all day and not get to the top of one of those hills."

"You've done it?"

"With my father. And I've not done it lately. For several years I've been away at school during hunting season."

He showed polite interest in her school, and she laughed at him. "You must think I'm retarded beyond help."

"And you're not, of course." His eyes seldom left her face.

"Well, not really. I was in medical school, and for that, you know, one ages."

He leaned toward her. "Why, that is fascinating!" he cried. "Tell me all about yourself!"

"Before *all* these people?" she challenged him.

It was fun to have a new man, and to like him. They rode, side by side, up the mountain, crossing the swift, icy streams, watching the footing—talking. Clancy Cobbins had thick brown hair, straight, and a bit long. He kept it in place with a knitted red cap which he pulled down to his ears when the wind became chill. When they stopped for the night, he offered to help Gretchen with her tent.

"No need. I have a sleeping bag, and will tuck under a pine tree."

Around the fire, replete with steak, potatoes, camp biscuits and fruit, the whole crowd talked about skiing.

"Do you have any long slopes?" asked Cobbins. "From what I've seen of your mountains, they have a tendency to sheer off into deep ravines."

"Not all of them," Til reminded him. "You simply must not forget Sun Valley."

"That's never mentioned around Vail," Clancy assured him.

They sang a little, they talked a little—and were ready to go to bed. The thin, cold air was like heady wine, and like wine, it made them sleepy.

The next day they walked up the mountain—and Clancy stuck close to Gretchen. "She's telling me about Idaho," he told someone who pointed this out.

"Oh, sure. What does she tell you?"

"Haven't you ever had instruction?"

"Not me. I'm still an innocent man."

This of course drew hoots of loud laughter. Clancy watched Gretchen and talked to her with new interest, mounting interest, and when they had picked up their horses on the downward trail, he again stayed close at her side or directly behind her. "Did you ride up with Holt?" he asked. "In his car?"

"Yes, I did. And two other people. Kathy Bennett and one of the men."

"I could manage to be the other man downhill, but . . . I'm bucking for a twosome."

She nodded. "It would be fun, but I won't drive a logging road. Can you?"

"I've never tried. Though I am used to mountains."

"They are one-truck wide in various places."

"I noticed that. I'd still like . . ."

She smiled at him and rode on. Below them, the lodge was in sight. She had always been a popular girl, and she was especially happy, just then, to have renewed the excitement of a new boy—or man, in this case—falling for her and showing that he had done so. Long ago she had become intrigued by the way different men showed their reactions to her. Some acted stunned, dumb, adoring. An occasional one—Til Holt, for example—set up defenses. "No blond broad is going to twist me around her finger!" declared some. That of course was a challenge for her to do a little twisting. With Til—mainly, she was trying to reach through his aloofness. He probably was entirely safe, but she must have a few hairs from his scalp. She had wanted to "reach" Holt as an antidote for what Valier had done to her pride. But the results had been much less than satisfactory. He admired Gretchen, perhaps he even liked her. But he still wanted to remain his own man, a bachelor.

While Clancy—he had no reservations whatever. "You are simply fabulous, Gretchen!" he had said to her. And meant it, which certainly did great things for any young woman's ego.

Kathy, Til Holt, the whole group, were watching this new attorney in town, and they were watching Gretchen. She herself felt some excitement about what would come next. Could he manage a "twosome" ride with her back to the valley?

No, he could not. Til and Jim Adams had organized the expedition, and things had worked out perfectly—no accidents, no complaints about food, nothing overlooked.

"We'll deliver you boy and girl scouts back to your front doors the way we brought you up here," said Til firmly.

"And let's get this flight off the ground!" added Jim, ex-air force, and still employed by the FAA, ready to command.

Clancy turned a wry face to Gretchen. "Shall we walk?" he asked.

"It would give us a lot of time to get acquainted," she said.

"But I can't just watch you disappear into Holt's car."

"I'm really sorry about that."

"I suppose you're in the phone book."

"My father is. I live at home."

"No office with *Dr. Purser* on the front door?"

"No."

"But of course you are busy."

"I work six hours a day in the hospital emergency room."

His face brightened. "Then you have time left over for dates? Dinner. Dim lights. Maybe even dancing?"

"Or a brightly lighted golf course. Though I should perhaps warn you, Counselor . . ."

He stepped closer. "I want to become involved," he said earnestly. "If you really are a maneater . . ."

"I'm not."

He laughed. "I was hoping you were. I'd bring my own salt and pepper." He glanced over his shoulder. "I'll say this in a hurry . . ."

"Jim's?"

"That's right. His hurry. But, first, I want to ask you for a date, anytime, anyplace. Will you, Gretchen? Oh, of course you will!"

She put her hand on the sleeve of his dark red jacket. "A real date, Clancy?" she asked.

"Yes. Why not? As real as I can make it."

She smiled brilliantly. "Ask your friends in Jim's car," she said. "It will take them the ride down to tell you why not."

She walked over to Til Holt's car, got in, and felt him start it immediately. "I thought we'd have to leave you behind," he growled.

"The new man in town—Clancy—was asking me for a date." Her lips prim, she fastened her seat belt.

Til negotiated the stretch of narrow, steep road. Then he glanced swiftly at Gretchen. He looked into the rear-view mirror. In the following car, Clancy was sitting beside Jim. Kathy and Jim's wife were in the back seat.

"He's a nice guy," he said sadly.

Gretchen stretched out. "I think so. A very nice grocer boy."

He drove along. "Gretchen," he said softly. "You wouldn't . . ."

She opened one eye. "Oh, yes," she said. "I think I would."

"Go back to sleep. I have to think about this."

"And tell the girls?"

"Later, maybe. Though if Clancy is saying *his* piece, I won't have to."

"Good night, Til. You had your chance."

"Which I took, dear heart. Which I took."

They drove for a couple of hours, and Gretchen actually did sleep. Now and then, Til would look at her. And considered telling the news to his back-seat riders. *Hoo boy!* The gang was in for a spell of . . .

He thought he'd better get this quiet time before the storm broke—as it could and would, all too soon.

It did break when the cars, by agreement, stopped in Jackass Bend—not actually the name of the place, but usually called that. There were toilet facilities, soda, coffee and beer. Sandwiches and snacks.

The cars converged, and the young people swarmed over the place, chattering, laughing. And demanding of Gretchen when the wedding would be.

Finally she put them off by reminding them that Clancy had not yet made good on his date offer.

They turned to that young man; his brown eyes were smiling, his poise complete. "The date will surely happen," he told Kathy Bennett. "And I can promise that whatever comes of it will be a pleasure."

Gretchen waved her hand, and with it the Coke bottle she was holding. Her hair shining, her cheeks pink from the sun and the exercise she had had, her denim jacket and bright scarf as becoming as any costume she had ever bought and worn, the women looked at her with rueful envy, the men with rueful admiration.

"You've got yourself a tiger by the tail," Johnny McLellan told Clancy. "Holt should-a told you that Gretch was a girl to take a gag seriously."

"So do I," said the newcomer. "I think Gretchen knows that."

If she had not guessed it, she soon found out about it. The thing had, she told him on their first date, started as a gag. "You can back out," she assured him, "and only the gag will be remembered."

He leaned forward across the small table where they were having dinner. "Do you want me to call it off?" he asked.

"I play fair . . ."

"All right. What about going down to Denver next weekend, and meeting my mother and father?"

Her eyes flared. "You are *serious!*" she gasped.

"Of course. My mother will call you."

She looked at him in wonder. She would go to Denver. She would wear her most becoming clothes, and be her most charming self . . .

She demurred somewhat more firmly when he produced a ring. "Oh, I couldn't!" she gasped.

He turned the white solitaire in his fingers so that it caught the light. "Don't you like it?" he asked. "Or—

don't you like me?"

"Why?" she cried, "I like you very much! And certainly you are persistent."

Clancy leaned back in the booth where, that evening, they were having a drink. "When I was sixteen," he said, "and fell hard for a girl, I would see her any chance I got. I would ride my bike up and down in front of her house. I would wait for a chance to see her on the street. I spent every penny I could scrape up on dates with her. She always got sick of me before the thing ended."

"Or another girl came along."

His eyes lifted to her face. "That never happened," he said. "I went away to prep school, her family moved away. When I was twenty, I went through the same thing with another girl. Then I thought I must marry her. Her people, and mine, had other ideas. But now— I've fallen hard for you, Gretchen. When first I saw you in that bunch of happy trail riders—the way you talked and laughed, the way you stood or rode your horse—I said, 'That girl's for me!' And the two days we had together . . . this week, since—I've fallen in love. I know you, I want you, I'd like to give you this ring."

She shook her head a little, but held out her hand. "If it fits."

"It will fit."

It did fit. His hand was strong and warm as it held hers. His kiss . . .

"*Wow!*" thought Gretchen. The man really was in love. And she found herself shaking. Trembling? Oh, but that couldn't be!

"I am going to speak to your father tomorrow," said Clancy.

She stared at him. "I didn't know men did that. I'm twenty-six years old, Clancy Cobbins!"

"And you are extremely fond of your father."

Well, yes, of course she was. "All right!" she said.

"I'm counting on his giving you anything you want," he said. His fine eyes were on her face. She gulped and turned the ring on her finger. "I'm not about to make a fool of you, Clancy."

"I hope not. So I'll see him tomorrow. And then we'll plan on that trip to Denver."

She shrugged. "You seem to have everything planned."

"And you don't like it?"

"I'm spoiled. I am sure our friends have told you that."

"They've told me."

"You should believe them."

"I contemplate a change in my life. I hope you will also make some adjustments. Leave your parents' home, make a home for me. Love me, let me love you . . ."

She shivered. This quiet-faced man, this strong man . . . "It's a beautiful ring," she said.

Clancy saw her father. Hugh Purser came home that evening and kissed his daughter. "We're going to have a wedding, Mamma," he told his wife.

"Ida B. said we were. She wants to plan it."

Gretchen jumped to her feet. "Over my dead body!" she cried.

"But, darling . . ."

"Don't worry," Gretchen advised her. "Tell us about your talk with Clancy, Dad."

"Well, he first made an appointment. He's a very attractive man, Mary. He came into my office, neatly dressed, ready to tell me about his own qualifications to be my daughter's husband."

Gretchen stared at him. "As—what?" she asked. "He's never told me."

"Well, the first thing he told me was that he was in love with you. I don't suppose you two have got beyond that."

Gretchen sat down. "There was that gag going 'round."

"I have no idea that Clarence Cobbins is marrying you against his will, sweetheart."

"Well, I don't suppose he is. Or would. He's proud of himself as a man."

"Which is good. He's a clever chap; others have told me. He will, in time, take over Tony Warrington's law practice. I—I hope you will marry him, Gretchen."

She got up and started across the room. "With you two men behind it," she laughed. "Seems as if Ida B. might be right. There's going to be a wedding. Kathy says I'm lucky."

"I think you well may be. Some men would just hold you to your promise and—"

Her eyes flared wide. "You don't think Clancy will?"

"Not against your will, I am sure."

No. She supposed he wouldn't. Though . . .

"Do you think, Dad—just suppose this thing did work out—that I could be good to him?"

"Why not?"

"Well, he's a nice guy. And I can be a rat."

"Oh, Gretchen!" He shook his head reprovingly.

She picked up a couch pillow and threw it down again.

"You should tell me that nobody is a rat unless she wants to be," she challenged.

He came to her. "I'll tell you one thing only," he said. "I like this man. Be sure, before you do anything concerning him."

Til Holt felt guilty about what seemed to be happening. He told Clancy that he did. "Don't let yourself be swept into anything because of something a silly girl said at a party."

"Gretchen is *not* a silly girl, Holt."

"She said a silly thing. That she would marry the first guy—"

Clancy put his hand on his friend's arm. "Let's get one thing straight, old man," he said. "I've fallen in love with Gretchen."

"Everybody falls in love with Gretchen, Clancy! I've done it myself."

Clancy's eyes sparked. "Well—I suspected that."

"Yes. But I—"

"Look, old man. If this wedding happens—and it will! I'll be marrying Gretchen. You'll find that out!"

"And she will?"

"Oh, yes. Certainly!"

Til studied the other man. "Should I envy you?"

"I don't know. I hope so."

Gretchen herself had qualms. She told Clancy that he didn't know her well enough to talk about marrying her.

"What don't I know?" he asked.

"Well, for one thing I am rotten spoiled. Maybe you've heard . . ."

"I've heard various things, yes."

"Perhaps you should listen to some of them."

"Look, Gretchen. Are you backing out of this? Seriously, I mean."

"Well, yes. At least, I'm trying to."

"Why?"

"Maybe because I am afraid."

He laughed gently. "That's allowed any bride, my darling."

"Oh . . ." She almost stuttered. "I was never bashful in my life!" she assured him.

"I was thinking of more substantial things."

"Like?"

"Trust. Faith. A promise given—"

"And kept." She turned the ring on her finger. "I'll keep this," she said slowly. "For a time. I'll go to Denver with you. But—"

"I want to tell my mother that you're the girl—"

"You may," she said quietly.

He looked surprised. "Then . . . ?"

"Because you're hurrying things, Clancy. Too much."

"But why should we wait? Surely you've had the candy, books, flowers courtship bit."

She laughed.

"And nothing ever happened."

"No, it didn't. And nothing may ever happen this time, Clancy."

"Oh, yes," he said firmly. "It will."

So she wore his ring. And she went to Denver to meet his parents. Driving from the airport to the house, she turned to him. "Clancy," she said earnestly. "Don't tell your mother you think you're going to marry me."

He glanced at her. Shining golden hair, soft fur,

carved wooden beads at her throat. "No?" he asked.

"No! It was a silly joke six weeks ago. Now—it's worn out. Done."

Swiftly his hand reached for hers. "That joke is not why I hope to marry you, Gretchen." His voice was deep.

"Oh!"

He smiled. As he did not—often.

She sank back in the seat. "Hmmmmn," she said. "I keep forgetting that I should be more careful out here in the mountains where men are men and we girls get ourselves fitted into that pattern. If we aren't careful. If we want to be careful."

She enjoyed her visit to Denver. Of course she already knew the city fairly well, and had friends there. Clancy's mother was a witty, dark-haired woman, small—and forthright in speech. She teased her son and Gretchen, mildly, about their coming. "Why don't you two just elope?" she demanded. "You're old enough to know what you want to do."

Gretchen and Clancy looked at each other.

"I'm proud of you, Mother," he said. "I wanted to show you to Gretchen, and Gretchen to you."

"Because you plan to marry."

Clancy shook his head. "Because I'd like you to be friends."

"We will be, but I am warning you both that I shall not wear a lace-yoked chiffon gown at your wedding."

Gretchen laughed aloud. "My mother will," she promised. "If all this comes to that."

"Won't it?" asked Mrs. Cobbins, her dark eyes widening.

"I don't know," said Gretchen. "Your son keeps telling me it will."

This gave Clancy's mother something to think about.

After dinner, the four played bridge. Clancy's father was a tall, scholarly quiet man, and he could play a steel-hard game. Gretchen was also acquiring some things to think about.

"She's very beautiful," she heard Mrs. Cobbins tell Clancy when Gretchen was going upstairs to bed.

"I can pick 'em!" said Clancy heartily.

When she tried to tell her own mother about the trip, Gretchen found that she could not make a good thing of the account. She described the home—a big, handsome rectangle of fieldstone, white pillars before the recessed entrance—the parents. Mr. Cobbins was a research chemist, Mrs. Cobbins—she was youthful, talky. Yes, she liked them.

"And they liked you, Gretchen?"

"Well, I hope so. They didn't believe I was an M.D."

"That's because you don't believe it yourself."

Gretchen turned on her mother. "Now don't you go being smart, too!" she cried.

"But, darling—"

"Everybody knows more about this whole thing than I do! Everybody tells me what is going on, and what is going to happen."

"Well, yes, they may seem to. We had Ida B. and Marcella for dinner while you were away."

"Good!"

"I know how you feel. But at ninety-six, Gretchen . . ."

"If she would just wash that handkerchief she holds

while taking food from her plate!"

"She enjoyed her dinner—though I served sweet potatoes, and she said she couldn't eat them."

"She won't eat anything with iron in it. Did you have other guests?"

"Oh, no."

"She called it a family dinner," said Hugh Purser from behind his newspaper. "And you don't have to worry a thing about your wedding, Gretchen. She has everything planned out for you."

"Do you suppose she will tell me?"

"She told your mother. She figures she is the power behind the throne."

"Somebody must be," said Gretchen dryly. "I certainly don't have much to say that gets listened to."

"Oh, sweetheart," cried her mother. "You know you are enjoying every minute of this."

At the time, Gretchen made no comment. Saying something about needing to convince the hospital that she was a doctor, she left the house. But she acknowledged to herself that the whole progression of events was intriguing. To see how a snowball could roll relentlessly downhill, gain momentum, be temporarily stopped by a shrub or rock, go around the obstacle, and bounce off again, getting bigger, and bigger . . .

Clancy was the motive force. She had never known such a determined man!

That morning, doing the things which Dr. Wagner had left orders for her to do—she took two case histories for new admissions, she responded to an emergency call and dressed the open wound—she did all sorts of routine things, and paid attention to what she was doing, but in between—walking swiftly down a corridor, changing her stained white smock for a fresh one—she thought about Clancy. He really was a nice guy, and handsome. His brown hair was fine, and smooth, his brown eyes were steady, warm, interested. He had good features, and a small dimple, or cleft, in his chin. For the trip to Denver he had worn a brown velvet jacket over a brown-figured shirt, very light tan slacks—good clothes, becoming clothes, but he had not thought about them. Once in a while he would smooth his hand back over his hair, otherwise he was interested, not in his appearance, but in what he was saying or doing, in what others were thinking. A concentrated man. Of course Gretchen was intrigued by him.

Did he excite her? Sometimes? Did she love him? How could she? Why didn't she? When she knew she would see him, when he touched her, or spoke in a certain intent way . . . Yes, she was intrigued. As she had never been by another man.

Valier? Oh, he had excited her, then angered her—but never intrigued or puzzled her. But Clancy—she would wait and see.

The town was intrigued, too, and their friends. They watched Gretchen; they watched the young lawyer, new in town. He was courting the girl, all right. And bets were laid as to the outcome. Other men had courted her, other men had found her beautiful. And nothing had come of it. But maybe, now, she did want to settle down, and had settled on this man for her purpose. This was the most popular theory about the situation.

Kathy Bennett, her closest friend, declared that this was the case. Gretchen was both charming and lovely, when she wanted to be. She knew a dozen ways to entrance a man. And having selected this eligible young chap she was using those ways, confident of what would happen.

She was a good catch . . .

Any man would find her physically desirable.

She had more to give a man than her beauty. Her father's wealth and prestige, her own status as a doctor —a man would be getting a bargain.

Clancy could have told these interested people that some of these factors made him inclined to hold back somewhat. Gretchen had told him that she was spoiled, and she was. She had told him that she usually got what she decided she wanted—she had told him about the silly joke, and warned him that he should not take advantage of that situation.

His line had been that he was his own man, and knew what he wanted to do. But was he his own man where Gretchen was concerned? Was any man with a beautiful woman whom he desired?

This bothered him . . .

He was still enchanted with her beauty, her quick and clever mind. He could laugh wholeheartedly when she cracked down on him about the puns he loved to make.

"Victor Hugo says puns are the droppings of a mind as it flies," she told him, facing him impudently, her chin out-thrust.

"I'm afraid of you when you're smart, Gretchen," he told her.

"Oh, good. I like men to be afraid of me."

He regarded her gravely. "No, you don't," he told her soberly. "And you don't want to be afraid of me."

"Clancy . . . ?"

He drew his car to the side of the road. They had been driving upward, and upward again, to the ski lodge and its runs. Now they were deep within the dark forests of spruce and pine; the mountains were all about them. To one side of the road ran the swift, green river, foaming white over a glistening black rock. Beyond it, set deep into the shadows, was a small log house, shuttered for the winter.

Clancy seemed to be studying it.

"People use these cabins in the summer," Gretchen told him uneasily. "They fish—enjoy the quiet. They usually plant a little garden . . ."

"Let's go look at it."

"Why?"

"Curiosity."

"It will be locked."

"I don't plan to break in. There's a footbridge up farther. Come on."

She was wearing ski gear, light blue. Stretch pants, a jacket, a tasseled knit cap back on her head. Skis were strapped to the car top.

"We'll be late," she reminded him.

He stood holding out his hand. Her lips set. Should she refuse to do this silly thing—or make him wish that he had not insisted on her doing it? She got out of the car. "I'm not wearing hiking shoes."

"We're not going to hike."

They crossed the bridge, they found deer tracks and those of small animals about the little house, and her hand on the latch swung the back door open. Clancy frowned; Gretchen was delighted. "We can go in," she cried. "Build a fire . . . and run no risk of breaking our leg on Bogus."

She did persuade him to go in. He said that he would leave a note to tell that they had been there. . . .

The house was clean, and well-stowed for winter. A bucket over the chimney pipe, mattress and pillows hoisted off the floor by thin wire, no food to tempt mice or ground squirrels. But there was a gasoline stove, and Gretchen set about making coffee.

Clancy watched her curiously. "Why?" he asked.

She studied his own clothes. Plaid jacket, corduroy trousers tucked into sturdy boots; his smooth, watchful face.

"Climb up and take the bucket off," she said. "I'm going to light the fire."

He shrugged, and did as she asked. When he came down again, she had released the pulley and dropped the mattress to the floor.

"How did you manage that?" he asked.

"I'm a rancher's daughter. I know about these things."

"Sometimes I wonder about what you know."

"In time, you'll find out," she said. She knelt, ready to light the fire. He came up behind her.

"It's snowing again."

"Is it?"

"And it will be black dark in an hour, long before we reach the lodge."

"If we go."

He took off his jacket, and unfolded a thick rug on the hearth. The fireplace was of stone, wide and deep. There was built into the hearth a square well which contained kindling, pine cones, and logs set on end. He lit the laid fire, lifted Gretchen to her feet and embraced her, kissed her.

She met him, laughing. "That was easy," she said impudently.

Going to look at the cabin had been his idea; she was willing to make it a better one.

The next morning, it took longer to get the cabin back as they had found it. Gretchen had found supplies and cooked breakfast, moving briskly, capably.

"You amaze me," he told her once.

"Why should I? Besides, we're going to be married . . ."

"Are we?"

"Oh, yes. Now we have to."

"Do we?"

"Yes, we do, Clancy. Don't you want to?"

"More than ever, Gretchen. But—"

She looked over her shoulder, laughing.

"It will be a marriage, Gretchen," he said sternly.

"Yes. Do you think I would have tricked you, if—"

"I think you did trick me. I think you would again. I think you are—that you would use me."

"Isn't that what you wanted?" she asked innocently.

He turned away, checking that everything was ready. He took the padlock from the nearby shelf and locked the door, then followed her across the doorward, across the little bridge to the car. In the night they had had an inch of snow, but the sun was coming up beyond their ravine.

As they drove away, Gretchen looked back at the snug little house sinking back into the shadows of the tall trees. She had traveled this road two dozen times in her life; this cabin had been here, but she had never seen it . . .

"Why?" she asked when they were a quarter mile on their way. "Why do you think I am using you?"

"I don't know. You have some reason. Maybe you have to prove something."

"You're a clever man, Clancy Cobbins."

"You've known that for some time. You know all that I am, Gretchen. I only wish—"

"That you knew me. But you don't, do you?"

"No, I don't. Not all of you, I am sure."

"Last night . . ."

"Don't be cheap!" He spoke sharply.

Her lovely, clear laughter bubbled between her lips. "You sound like a husband."

"I feel like a husband. Yours."

"And that now you must marry me."

"I've felt that way for the past month."

Should she tell him that she had felt that way, too? Now.

"Last night, I was in love with you. I am today."

She sat back in the car seat. "I know that," she said soberly.

"Then—we'll be married."

"And you'll study me."

"No, I'll love you, and you'll learn what that can mean."

For the rest of the drive, for all that day, that evening, and for all the next day, she kept stealing glances at this man, remembering his kisses, his touch, his warm strength, and yet there was his almost stern gravity now. He had submitted gracefully enough to her seduction, but second thoughts must now be holding him, or was it the daze of realization?

She was not a promiscuous woman, and never had

been. The brief experience with Valier had taught her many things. This was—different. This man was different. Somehow she did not believe that he was dazed, and the thought alone excited her. His lips, his hands—

Had she managed the swift, hot hour in the firelight? Or had Clancy planned the whole thing? The cabin, the stop— Had he planned the ski trip itself to accomplish —what he had accomplished? Had he? *Had he?*

That thought, too, excited her, and she let her emotions take over. Even anger swept through her. How Victorian could a person get? "Now you have to marry me."

Well, she did not have to! She certainly did not. Though, of course, now she wanted to. Clancy was a very exciting man! She was tempted to ask him about the cabin he had "picked" and conveniently found unlocked. He would answer her if she did ask him. He would tell her.

But she sighed. She was pretty sure she would never get the courage to ask him.

When he brought her home on Sunday night and unpacked their gear from his car, she heard him say something to her father about the ski lodge dormitories. "Next trip, we'll have been married," he said firmly.

Her father said something.

"Oh, yes," said Clancy. "Gretchen promised she would."

Well, she had. At that dumb party two months ago. And thirty-six hours ago, the promise had been repeated. "We're going to be married," she had said.

"Me and my dumb mouth!" she scolded herself.

The position in which she found herself was untenable. If she had just kept still! She would have met Clancy, she could have flirted with him, charmed him, flattered him. The end results would have been the same.

And her friends, especially Kathy Bennett, would not be talking about Gretchen and her "grocer boy."

Though, to her amusement and dismay, she herself sometimes called him that. The "grocer boy" had given her a ring, she had a date with the "grocer boy" for the performance of the Icecapades.

"If I thought you and Clancy were serious . . ." mused her pretty little mother.

"Did you ever see Clancy when he wasn't serious?" Gretchen challenged her.

"How about you?"

"Oh, yes. I'm serious. I plan to marry him."

"When?"

Her daughter shrugged.

"Gretchen . . . ?"

She hugged her mother. "I thought before Christmas."

CHAPTER 4

THE PURSERS invited Mr. and Mrs. Cobbins to come up for the next weekend, and, at a dinner, they announced the engagement of the "young people," and the wedding date.

It was a very gay party. Gretchen looked ravishing in an off-the-shoulder ruffled gown of deep red taffeta, rustling and seductive.

"It ain't gonna work," declared Til Holt. He said it to Clancy.

"State your bet," said his friend. "By the way, will you be my best man?"

"I wouldn't miss it for a farm in the valley."

"But you still don't approve."

"Oh, it isn't a matter of approval. I just think you've got the wrong girl."

"You could have had her yourself, Kathy tells me."

Til laughed aloud. "Then I have a great deal to thank you for. And certainly I will be your best man."

Gretchen even found time to take Clancy's hand and go talk to Ida B. enthroned in a chair beside a small table against the wall.

The old lady was delighted. She had the wedding all planned, she assured Clancy.

"Does it include me?"

She slapped at him playfully with her old claw of a hand.

Beyond her, Marcella, the niece, giggled shrilly. Clancy glanced her way. "Mrs. Willis?" he asked.

"Miss," said the large woman. "By choice!" She came toward him. She wore a turban of striped blue silk; and tonight an ancient fur stole hung from her shoulders. Mrs. Callier wore a mink jacket, though the house was warm enough . . .

"I know Gretchen will have a church wedding," said the old lady, "and I think she should wear white velvet."

"That would be beautiful," murmured Clancy.

"Oh, it would be!" cried Gretchen. "With a full train, Ida B.? White velvet, edged with white fur, and sequin-embroidered in a design of lilies . . ."

Clancy touched her arm. "Don't, dear," he protested.

"I'm sorry," she whispered. She leaned toward the old lady, who sat clutching her fur jacket like a security blanket. "You go on making your plans," she said. "For all I know, things will work out your way."

She walked away from Mrs. Callier; she walked the length of the room, her eyes blazing, her golden hair swinging against her shoulders.

"Now what was that all about?" asked her friends, watching her.

"He told her to shut up, and she did."

"That's never happened before."

"And she won't wear white velvet when she's married, either."

"Did she say she wouldn't be married in the church?"

"Personally, I doubt if she plans to be married at all."

"Do you think someone should tell Clancy?"

"You do it!" said her companion. "I bruise easy."

"So will he . . ."

"If she stands him up, you mean."

"That, or even if she marries him."

And there was another ripple of laughter across the chattering group. "You girls do love her, don't you?" said Til Holt.

"It's a matter of give and take, Til," one of Gretchen's friends instructed him. "She plays the game, too."

Everyone agreed that Gretchen and Clancy made a handsome couple. Everyone liked the Cobbinses from Denver. But few tongues left the cheeks when the Pursers' friends talked about the projected marriage.

"I am glad," said one woman, prominent in town—her husband was big in real estate—"I am glad this lawyer is not my son."

"Your son, Poppy," said the person talking to her, "is already married, with four children."

"Ha! That wouldn't stop Gretchen if she thought she wanted him."

"You know what I think? I think Gretchen doesn't know *what* she wants. Not really."

Interest and speculation grew, and the marriage plans proceeded. Too many plans, too many things to be considered. Yes, Gretchen agreed, Kathy could be her maid of honor. "If she's sober."

"Gretchen!"

"Well, Mom, she—"

"She's your friend, your best friend, and always has been."

"That started because you and Dad, and the Bennetts, did everything together. You still do. Kathy and I shared baby sitters, we shared paper dolls and birthday parties —now I suppose she just about has to— What does Til Holt keep saying? She'll 'stand up' with me. What a filthy term! Why can't Clancy and I go off and get ourselves married? I don't want a big wedding, and invitations, and nasty little napkins marked Gretchen and Clarence. Nobody calls him *Clarence!*"

There were parties. Two showers. The church women and her mother's bridge clubs gave luncheons. These things played hob with her hospital hours. She apologized to Dr. Wagner.

"Take a couple of months off," he suggested.

"I thought maybe I was being useful here."

"You are. But when you're tired . . ."

"Oh, golly, yes! I'm tired all the time. There are so many things to fight over!"

The doctor laughed. "You don't mean *fight.*"

"I most certainly do. Did you ever go against the will of Ida B. Callier?"

"Heavens, no!"

"Well, keep it that way. And why should my father insist on my meeting with Jonah IntVeld so that he can tell me about stocks and stuff? Why do I need to be given such things?"

"Because your father wants to establish your security."

"I'll be secure. I have my profession, Clancy has his. Besides, why can't Dad do the instructing?"

"It's Jonah's specialty. Estate planning."

Gretchen groaned.

"Don't you like Jonah?"

"Oh, sure. Everybody likes Jonah. And I really do love his wife."

"Dolly, yes. Hypertension."

"Oh, *Doctor!*"

"You should be concerned, too."

"I am. I am. But just now . . ."

"Take the two months, Gretchen. Where are you and Cobbins going to live?"

"Probably not together. I say we should stay with the folks . . ."

"Oh, no! Never."

"That's what Clancy says, and I'm pretty sure Dad agrees with him. That's what we fight about. All of us. I don't see why we couldn't just stay on in that big house—"

"But you aren't going to," said the doctor.

"I'm beginning to think we are not. Maybe we should just abandon the whole project."

"I hope you're joking."

Gretchen hoped she was, too. Though there were times . . .

The dismay she had felt from the beginning of this matter of marrying Clancy was growing very fast, and deepening day by day. Each point that came up and had to be decided seemed to add another thread, another cord . . .

By now she was so bound up in the whole thing—her father's financial settlement, her mother's gift of a cameo pin which she had worn at her own wedding, this latest decision about where she and Clancy would live.

Alone. Together. Surrounded by all the glittery wedding gifts . . . "If I get one more table broiler, I'll open a restaurant!" Gretchen declared, and her family laughed at her.

But those broilers meant something—this situation had gone so much farther than she had thought about . . . Did Clancy feel the same way?

She asked him.

"I understand premarital doubts are entirely normal, Gretchen."

"Should we call the whole thing off?"

"Would you want to go through all this with some other man?"

"What other man?"

"I don't have a candidate. And I certainly don't have anyone to take your place."

"I see. If we get married at all, this might as well be it."

He chuckled. "It had better be us," he told her. Those times she was thrilled, and thought she must love the man.

Those times, standing with him, looking up at him, as they said good night in the hall of her father's home, the light of the chandelier casting a shadow of his head across her face, she would return his kiss warmly, and even cling to him. Those times were very good.

Unless she used his warmth, his urgency, to speak again of her wish to live on in this house. "We could just go up these stairs . . ." she said softly.

He dropped his hands, he lifted his head, and went over to the door. "No, Gretchen," he said. And firmly. "No."

She was surprised at his firmness; always she had been

able to get, to ask and to get, agreement from others. Well, not from Valier, she remembered. But that experience made it all the more important that she now persuade Clancy . . .

She would try. She did try.

And Clancy continued to be firm. "We'll start with a little house, Gretchen," he said. "There are some attractive ones in the Highlands."

"Miles from town."

"Yes. Then there are those new apartments . . ."

There were. Built to overlook the city, with a long vista of river and mountains.

"I've never lived in an apartment."

He laughed. "You've never been married before. I think maybe you'll like both experiences."

"The idea of an apartment horrifies me."

"Oh, Gretchen!"

"But it does, Clancy. To think of other people, strange people, above me, around me— Please, Clancy? We could have a whole suite of rooms here."

"No, Gretchen."

She coaxed, and she offered again to call the whole thing off.

But she found him firm. They must decide, he told her, by the time he got back from the trip he was taking to Salt Lake City with Susan Warrington.

She stared at him. "Two weeks before you marry me, you're going off with Susan?"

He laughed at her. "It's about her husband's estate, Gretchen."

"A likely story."

"But a true one. I'm her attorney, and attorneys often

have to take trips concerning a client's affairs."

"Especially if that client is someone like Sue."

"She's quite a girl!"

"You've noticed that."

"Oh, sure. She was one reason I came into the Warrington office. Til Holt says I missed a bet, not marrying that rich widow."

Gretchen looked at him warily. He could have married Susan. He could, even now.

So jealousy became a part of this new experience. Jealousy, and even fear. What if Clancy should decide . . . ?

His three-day absence gave her time to think, and to speak to her father about Clancy's determination that they have their own home. "He talks about apartments. I'd rather stay here, make the south bedroom into a sitting room—"

Her father smiled at her indulgently.

"We'd love to have you here with us," said her mother.

But her father, she could tell, did not agree.

"What should I do, Dad?" Gretchen asked him.

"Do as he says, or don't marry him." He spoke reasonably.

This attitude shocked her. Not to marry Clancy would be another failure. In everyone's eyes. Especially in her own. Proof that she had not managed things well. Everyone would know that she had failed. But, most important, she herself would know it.

That afternoon she took a long drive, alone, with snow piled into a four-foot wall at the side of the road. But she wanted to debate this with herself, and decide what to do. She had publicly vowed she would marry Clancy—the *grocer's boy*. There had been many times when she knew that she could love the man who happened to be that *boy*. So—

Besides, she would, she knew, hate to see another woman get Clancy. He was a very solid, a very attractive, man.

And her release of him would stir things up among the ladies. *Wheee!* Wouldn't it just! Kathy—and Susan Warrington. Kathy was no threat, but Clancy liked Susan.

And, as he had pointed out, where could Gretchen do better?

She found a place to turn the car, and she drove back to town.

When Clancy called that evening, she told him that she had rented one of the apartments downtown.

A week before Christmas, they were married, with only the two families present in the church, and "everybody and his cat" invited to the reception at the Purser home. There were flowers—freesia and Talisman roses—all over the place, the buffet was lavish, and champagne flowed like water. Til Holt was just about as beamingly enchanted as was Ida B. Callier.

About everything. The food, the beautiful home—the exceedingly dressed-up guests. "More than would come to my funeral," declared Hugh Purser, and his wife assured him that it was bad luck to speak of death at a wedding.

"What bad luck could those two have?" he asked, gazing across the room at Gretchen and her "grocer's boy." She called him that, gayly, and was beautiful. "Radiant," said Mrs. Cobbins. "White satin, after all, is the only right thing for a bride. I'm glad our son is so in love with her."

And Clancy really did love her, Gretchen decided. Which should hold her, she told her mirrored self as she changed her satin, lace and pearls for the green worsted suit and the fur jacket which she would wear to go away with Clancy.

CHAPTER 5

IMMEDIATELY, Gretchen found that she liked being married to Clancy—and that she did not like living in an apartment. She went back to work, part time, at the hospital, and by their second wedding anniversary, she and Clancy had built a home against the slope of a tree-covered mountain. A combination of wide stretches of glass, old brick, and wood, it sat far back from the street, and the approach to it was through a garden court, with rock and shrubbery landscaping and paths of Mexican beach pebbles. Two tall pines stood like totem poles before the house.

Gretchen had been enchanted with all that went into the building of a home; for a year she lived tile and paint and fabric samples, doorknobs and copper pipes, the slope of a roof. All these things could fill every corner of her life.

"There's so much *to* it!" she cried happily.

The young couple had undergone the usual prying questions. "No babies, Gretchen?"

"Not quite," said Gretchen. "We're building a house!"

Clancy heard her, laughed, and agreed. "That's what we're doing," he confirmed. "With a roof of hand-hewn shakes."

Gretchen had wanted to buy the log cabin on the river road, and build around it.

Clancy vetoed the idea. It was too far from the city; there was no piped-in water, no sewer. They could find a satisfactory situation at the edge of town, and they did find it, tucked under one of the "benches." And there they built the long low house of mellowed brick, rough-finished cedar planks, with the pole-pine trees framing the scarlet-red front door. And a fireplace of local stone, as like the one in the cabin as Gretchen could remember, including the sunken stone well in the floor to hold kindling sticks, pine cones, and a half-dozen logs, stood on end.

"I have married a sentimental woman," announced Clancy.

Gretchen smiled at him. "Didn't you know you were doing that?"

"Frankly, no, I didn't."

"I knew you were one. A sentimentalist."

"Well, so did I know *that!*"

Gretchen nodded. "I think we're going to like our house," she promised.

"I've enjoyed it already, for the past months, seeing you happy, and busy—"

"And we'll be out of the—the *blasted*—apartment!"

"Millions of people live in apartments."

"Perhaps I should point out that I am not millions of people."

"I guessed as much the first time I saw you."

* * *

The house was finished, decorated and furnished, and Gretchen enjoyed being a gay hostess in it. She still enjoyed the prestige awarded her as an M.D., though she did not, really, practice. She gave time to the hospital, but she had never established her own office. The community, she argued, had sufficient medical service; they had a good hospital and at least two excellent doctors on the staff, with others not so good, and Gretchen to fill in as required.

There were those who would have argued with her on these points, but she would say little to defend her position. She need not point out that she was married, with the obligations that went with that status. Her husband was "nice," he was kind, and thoughtful, loving. But he was busy, a young man on his way up.

All of these things were known to Gretchen, if not publicly acknowledged. And, in case she did not know, they were listed for her, in Clancy's slightly embarrassed presence, on the Sunday afternoon when Ida B. Callier and her niece drove out to the Cobbinses' new home so that Ida B. could tell Clancy, formally, that he was, from then on, to be her attorney.

"She came out here to snoop!" Gretchen whispered fiercely to Clancy when he started to show the house to their callers.

"Everybody else has come, one way or another," said Clancy. "You should have invited her."

It was slow progress, what with the walker and Mrs. Callier's willingness to advise. They should have deeper padding under the carpets . . .

"You'd have more trouble walking," said Gretchen.

"I'd get one of those big mural panels for behind your bed," said Ida B.

She approved of their formal dining room.

"Mother furnished it," murmured Gretchen.

But they should have a railing around the small, sunny deck outside the family room.

"It's less than a foot off the ground," Gretchen pointed out.

"You still could step off." The old lady peered up at the foothill behind the house. "I hope one of those rocks doesn't come down on you," she said.

Gretchen exchanged glances with Clancy.

All in all, though, Ida B. approved of the house. They established her in the family room, and listened to her talk for twenty minutes about her own abilities as a house planner. "I should have been an architect," she admitted. "I wake up at night and plan how things should be. I keep telling Marcella that I want to build a new house."

"And I keep telling her she's crazy," said Marcella quietly.

"I could do it," declared Ida B. "That's why I came clear out here, Clancy. To tell you that I want you to handle all my legal work, and—"

"Could you come to the office in a day or two?"

"Oh, my records and papers and things are all in Tony Warrington's files. If anything comes up, you can come to the house. I just thought, since Gretchen is my doctor . . ."

Gretchen gasped. "I'm not anybody's doctor, Mrs. Callier," she said firmly.

Ida B. smiled patiently. "But of course you are, dear.

You took care of my dizzy spells."

"But I am not practicing. You must not depend on me."

"If I get sick, you'll know it. I don't know if you call it practicing, but you work at the hospital. And I read in the paper where you and the other doctors go to the Four County Medical Society meetings."

"Dr. Wagner and Dr. Tipton go, yes," Gretchen agreed. "I sometimes attend."

Sometimes it was fascinating to see the way Ida B. could spread her net and catch one up.

"Do you have fun?"

"Well, yes, I enjoy the meetings. The men want to establish some sort of mobile clinic service to go up into the hills on a regular basis. And the dinner meetings are always more social than they are medical. Even Clancy has gone to a couple."

"And I know he made a hit!" cried Marcella in her foolish way.

"He is popular everywhere," said Gretchen primly. Clancy laughed aloud.

"And," said Mrs. Callier, "I want him to tell me what is happening with Sue Warrington."

A chilling silence fell on the room. "What sort of happening, Mrs. Callier?" asked Clancy quietly.

"Oh, don't talk like a lawyer to me!"

"But you just said—"

"And you told me to come to the office for legal matters."

He looked with new respect at the old lady. Ninety-six, and able to hold her own in a situation such as she herself had created.

"I'm sorry, Mrs. Callier," he said firmly, "but I really cannot discuss one client's affairs with another."

Mrs. Callier felt of the beads at her throat, she picked up her pocketbook and laid it down again. "I would like to know the truth about the stories going around town, Mr. Cobbins," she said primly. "I've heard enough . . . that a cousin of Tony Warrington's is living in her house. Folks are sure—at least they are *afraid*—he is after Sue's money. I think he may do her physical harm and make off with some of the diamonds and her car; she owns valuable furs, too."

Gretchen leaned forward. Clancy held up a warning hand to silence her.

"You must not think, Mrs. Callier," he said, "because you consider me your attorney that I would . . ."

"You are her attorney, too. You would know the truth."

Clancy sighed, and for a minute sat thoughtful.

"He's smart," thought Gretchen, watching him. "But he's young, too. Against old harpies like Ida B. he could have a hard time, and say the wrong thing, if only to give her the material to carry around town. She and Marcella."

Clancy lifted his chin. "I came here two years ago," he said firmly. "A little more than that. I came in to help in the law office where Mr. Warrington had been a senior partner. He had died suddenly. Because of his prestige and his large practice, there was a great deal of work left undone at the time of his unexpected death. I knew the man only slightly in person, though of course I was well acquainted with his reputation."

Mrs. Callier listened quietly, a smug smile lifting her

badly rouged lips; now and then, as Clancy talked, she nodded in agreement. Her hair was dressed in dozens of tiny curls, tinted lavender, and scattered thinly over her head, around the edge of a small flowered hat, the flowers crushed and dusty-looking. Mrs. Callier still wore the fur coat in which she had come into the warm house.

"They'd better bury her in a mink jacket," Gretchen's father had one time said, "or Ida B. won't go."

Now this old, old woman sat watching Clancy, listening eagerly to what he was saying, or might say, her whole manner sly, waiting.

Clancy was telling that he was taking care of legal matters concerning the Warrington estate. "But I can't talk about Mrs. Warrington, Mrs. Callier. You should not want me to. There is surety for you in knowing that I don't discuss our clients."

He was pleasant, he was firm. And after another half hour, the two women departed, Clancy going out with them to their car. Then he stood watching Marcella lurch down the road toward town.

"She's a terrible driver," he told Gretchen when he came inside again. "*Brrrr!* It's cold out there!"

He picked up a book and settled in a deep, soft chair beside the fire. Gretchen moved about, restlessly, changing the positions of three pottery bowls on the chimney shelf, moving a woven Indian basket, gathering up the day's newspaper and taking it out of the room, coming back with two apples, one of which she put into Clancy's outstretched hand. She sat down on the low coffee table and gazed into the fire.

"Tell me," she said softly.

Clancy's eyes lifted and smiled. She was wearing a white blouse, coral knit slacks, with a coral scarf tying back her golden hair. "Tell you what, beautiful?"

"Flattery will get you far," she told him, "but I'll still ask you about Sue Warrington and the story Ida B. wanted."

"And didn't get, I might point out."

"She probably already knew more about it than you do."

"Then why . . . ?"

"She wanted to be able to say, 'Clancy Cobbins told me so-and-so.' "

"I see." He picked up the book.

"Clancy—"

"Haven't you heard the gossip?"

"Bits and whiffs. I, too, want the truth."

"What's your reason?"

"Not to name-drop. Nor to repeat."

He regarded her gravely.

"If you don't tell me," said Gretchen, throwing her apple core into the fire, where it hissed and shriveled, "I'll get that mural for over your bed."

"I'll move into the plaid guest room if you do."

"You wouldn't like it, dear. So—"

"All right. But I trust you know the term 'privileged communication,' and 'off the record,' *and* how to keep your lip buttoned?"

She nodded. "I know them. And truth really is better than gossip, Clancy."

"Not always. In this case, you can decide for yourself."

She hugged her arms around her knees. And waited.

"About a month ago," said Clancy slowly, "Susan told me that this man had come to her house in the late afternoon . . ."

"Attractive?"

Clancy frowned. "I don't know. Not to me, but—"

"And he was Tony's cousin."

"I don't think he was anybody's cousin. But he *said* his name was Warrington. He called himself Colonel Warrington, said that he had been a POW, and that he was planning to enter our Junior College to get his Master's degree."

"At the *Junior College?* They don't give . . ."

Clancy lifted his hand. "He didn't tell Sue what he would be studying. But he did say he would like to rent a room from her . . ."

"So he could do her in and steal her white beaver coat."

"Maybe that was his idea. Anyway, Susan said she couldn't rent him a room, and finally got rid of him. The next day she told me about him and asked if there was any record of such a cousin."

"And there wasn't."

"Not that I can find."

Gretchen's soft lips formed the word *lawyer* silently, and Clancy chuckled.

"But while I was checking the file on Judge Warrington," he continued, "Tom Benny dropped into the office." He looked inquiringly at Gretchen.

"I know him," she said. "Real estate, insurance—"

"Yes. His wife is a salesman, too. Sales *person.*"

"That she is!"

"Yes. And it seems that this same character—now reduced to Lieutenant Colonel—had come into their office and asked Mrs. Benny about buying a house. Something in the forty-five to fifty thousand range."

"*Wheeee!*" said Gretchen.

"A-hmmmmn. So Mrs. Benny took him around to see a place or two; he explained who he was, that he was transferring his bank account here from Los Angeles. He selected one place he liked—"

"Which house?"

"Oh, Greta!"

"It's all part of a fascinating story."

"Yes. Fascinating. Well—he told Mrs. Benny that he had deposited a large amount of money in the bank—transferring an account he had had in Portland—"

"Why Portland?"

"I have no idea. Then he borrowed two dollars in cash from her, and promised to make a down payment on the house as soon as his certified check had cleared."

"Then he went away. Where?"

"Well, he turned up next at a Rotary Club meeting. Again he was Colonel Warrington, and he said he was going to live in the Warrington home as an heir. He said he was somewhat disabled, and could claim that much from Sue. That's where I came into the picture. The man had told her the same thing. She had come home late in the afternoon and had found him asleep on her living room couch."

Gretchen looked amazed. "How had he . . . ?"

"Sue's maid had let him in. Because . . ."

"Because he said he was a cousin. And he must be attractive."

Clancy laughed and shook his head. "But that is where I came in. Sue called me, I got a police officer and went out to the house."

"Is that one of the times you broke a date with me to do something for Sue? And *with* her?"

"It could have been."

"And you would not have told me unless I had insisted on hearing Ida B.'s gossip."

Clancy picked up his book.

"All right, all right," agreed Gretchen. "I'm jealous, but I can rise above it. Go on. What happened next?"

"Well, we got the man out of Sue's house. We got the proper writs prohibiting his return there, forbidding his harassment of her. We asked for his military papers—"

"And he was not a colonel!"

"He was not. He had seen service, and had recently been discharged from a veterans' mental-care facility."

"Oh, my. And his name wasn't Warrington?"

"Well, yes, it was. By adoption. He had, as a small child, been adopted by a family named Warrington, and his foster father, in fact, was about a fourth cousin of the Judge's."

"Is he an heir?"

"No way. In fact, he's back in a veterans' hospital—I persuaded him to go voluntarily—and I doubt if we'll hear from him again. Sue wanted to do something for him, but I would not allow it. There's no reason she should. And it certainly would invite similar claims. Tony Warrington was related to half the people in this part of the country."

Gretchen nodded. "I know. I think even he and Dad shared a great-grandmother."

"I'll bet. Well, there's your story."

"Why couldn't you tell Ida B.?"

"Because it was none of her business, and because of the less-than-accurate way she would repeat it."

"I see. I suppose Sue is grateful to you."

"Gretchen . . ."

"I'm jealous," she agreed. "As you have pointed out, she is pretty, she is rich. And I'll get us some dinner."

For several minutes, Clancy sat thoughtful. Then he mended the fire and went out to the kitchen. Gretchen was moving about. She had steaks on the broiler, a pan simmering on the stove, and she was tearing lettuce for a salad. She looked up at him inquiringly.

He straddled one of the counter stools.

"I was going to set up a table before the fire," she said.

"You still can." He reached for a bit of lettuce. "About Susan Warrington," he said. "I feel I have to protect her, Greta. She's a grand person, you know, and that estate is a big, complicated job to be dumped on her."

"And you should have married her," said Gretchen, ducking down into a low cupboard for a cruet of vinegar.

"Well, now," said Clancy. "I am not entirely convinced of that."

"No?" asked Gretchen.

"Not entirely," said Clancy. "Why don't we eat here on the counter?"

They could talk together, Gretchen and Clancy. They enjoyed doing many things together. The town, their friends, said that they were really getting along fine.

No one could deny that they seemed to be. They played golf, though seldom together. But they did play bridge together. Clancy's parents had taught him well, and he and Gretchen helped organize a duplicate club. They went skiing, and boating in the summer. They did all the social things a popular young couple could do.

Clancy conducted his busy law practice, Gretchen worked, as needed, at the hospital. She served as physician for the blood bank visits to the town; she served in a similar capacity for the school immunization programs. It was through these free-will services that she and Clancy became rather special friends with Jonah and Dolly IntVeld.

These people—a lot of people said they were special. They did good works—Red Cross, church work, charitable projects. Dolly served at the well baby clinic, Jonah was treasurer for the United Fund—but they also gave parties and attended those given by others. They always were part of the gayest group. Clancy and Gretchen were younger by twenty years, but in one way and another they became very close friends.

They planted rose gardens together. They went to San Francisco for a concert series. They dropped in casually on each other . . . It was a good friendship—which also surprised the town.

Dr. Wagner mentioned this at one of the medical society meetings. "You must have things in common," he decided.

"Dolly and Jonah are great people," said Gretchen.

"I don't dispute that. But you and Clancy—"

"We're trying to be great, too. Maybe?"

"Don't get sassy with me, girl."

"All right. I won't. Well, I've considered the point you have in mind. And I've decided that differences can help in a relationship. Different ages, tastes, opinions, they can help form a strong friendship. Just as they can strengthen a marriage."

Dr. Wagner regarded her with respect.

"They give you things to talk about," Gretchen explained.

"Yes. They would do that."

"Clancy lets me go to these meetings with you. No, he won't take me, or let me drive off alone—so you're stuck."

"I enjoy your company."

"Mhmmmn. How does your wife feel about it?"

"She's jealous, of course, but she says she expects to be, since she married a doctor."

Gretchen laughed. "I don't think Clancy is jealous," she said. "In fact, I met Jim Adams in the lobby before we came in here, and he asked me why I wasn't at the country club bash. He said he was sure he had seen Clancy there with Til Holt, Susan Warrington, and others."

"Didn't you know he was going?"

"I knew there was a party."

"And you're not jealous?"

"Well, sure I'm jealous. I'll tell Clancy so, too, when I see him."

Dr. Wagner laughed. "If you'd take your M.D. more seriously," he said mildly, "maybe Clancy would, as well. He thinks you're just dabbling in it now, that you aren't really interested in the time element for gall bladder surgery."

Gretchen made a face. "I do enjoy these meetings . . ." she said.

"All right, then. Enjoy them. You can go to a country club bash on the other thirty days of the month."

"And not take my jealousy seriously."

"Does Clancy?"

"No. No, he doesn't."

All these things Gretchen did, and enjoyed. No one who watched her said, or probably thought, that she was tired of her housekeeping and the interests typical of such a young woman with time and energy to spare.

"She should doctor full-time," said some of her interested observers, "since evidently she doesn't plan on children."

If these recommendations were made to Gretchen, she probably thought her friends should be satisfied when she was elected Glamor President of the Four County Medical Society.

This election was impressively announced at the society's annual dinner, the third after Gretchen's marriage. That night she was truly glamorous in a gold-frosted caftan of brilliant blue chiffon.

It was a very exciting evening; most of the doctors beamed about their new president, though some were cynical. "It would be better if she ever got down to swabbing throats and taking blood pressures," Clancy overheard one man grumble.

Clancy was inclined to agree but volunteered no opinion to Gretchen. Time had a way of straightening things out for her. Her parents were proud, and Gretchen thrived on the excitement. She took the society meetings seriously, and checked on the programs planned.

And it certainly was during her year as president that the Mobile Office project was finally developed and established. Discussion of this project and the raising of funds for its implementation had been going on for some time before Gretchen, as president, could announce its accomplishment, could tell the schedule whereby the trailer would be stationed at five designated small towns in the district, each of them for three hours of the early afternoons on specified days. Two doctors from the society, one of them from the hospital staff, would be on duty. The hospital itself would be the supervising organization.

The hospital—especially Dr. Wagner and Dr. Tipton—was proud of the project. They asked Gretchen to work out the monthly schedule for doctors to attend the Mobile Office, and its location. Quite a lot of pictures and columns of articles were printed about the shining trailer, with its red cross on both sides and the top, parked beside the IOOF Hall in one village, in a fenced-in pasture of another, in the town square of still another . . . Nurses from the hospital were volunteering their services.

"It shows," said Gretchen happily, in all the interviews, "that when doctors really want to, they can give medical care to smaller communities."

The trailer consisted of two rooms—a small one, seven by eight feet, which served as consultation and examining room, and a combination lab and waiting room, eleven by eight feet, furnished with chairs, a small stove and oil heater, electric lights, a sink and closets and cabinets. The Four County Medical Society was named on a sign that ran the length of one side. And in any account of the trailer, Gretchen, as president, always was featured, her picture published. White lab coat, black bag, and smile.

"Photogenic, isn't she?" was one mild remark when articles and pictures came back to the city, to the hospital, to her friends.

Jonah IntVeld secured a blow-up of one of these pictures, asked Gretchen to autograph it, and hung it in his office.

Til Holt praised the project and Gretchen in his weekly broadcast as City Manager, and promised to have Dr. Cobbins appear with him soon on the program.

Clancy boldly labeled a drawer in the family room storage wall "CLIPPINGS," and stuffed it with the material available.

Gretchen herself glowed under all the praise and excitement.

"Does she deserve the credit she's getting?" various people asked Dr. Wagner.

"No, not really," said that honest, hard-working man. "But it certainly helped us to have a female president of the society. Many more pictures are taken of her, and published, than ever would be for the rest of us medical buzzards."

"Does she work with the Mobile Office?"

"Oh, yes, she takes her turn."

"But she doesn't work regularly at the hospital, she doesn't have her own office, does she?"

"Well, no."

"Why doesn't she work at being a doctor?"

Dr. Wagner shrugged. "She may, sometime. I expect she will."

Clancy asked Gretchen this same question one evening when she had come home late from trailer duty, still wearing her white coat. "You're smart," he told her.

"I know just how much you've given to this project. You're probably a very good doctor. Why don't you work at it?"

"I'm tired tonight, Clancy."

"Did you have lots of patients?"

"No. I mean, about twenty came in. But I didn't do it all. There was Dr. Giamonco, and the nurse."

"Giamonco, eh? Do you want to go someplace for dinner?"

"Could we?"

"Of course. And you can answer my question instead of warming up yesterday's stew."

While she changed, he stood gazing up through the skylight at the wooded mountainside behind the house. The late sun was casting blue shadows among the trees and gilding their tops. Gretchen had wanted skylights—one here in the family room, one in their bedroom—so she could "watch the mountain." Clancy enjoyed the view as much as she did. Tonight, he found himself relaxing the tension with which he had met her return home.

He loved her, he was proud of her—

They ate dinner in the formal dining room of the old Victorian hotel downtown. High ceilings, oak paneling, dim portraits, and excellent food made the place popular; they met some friends, and a lot of people recognized them. Gretchen relished the comments which followed their progress to a small table in an alcove.

"I thought you were tired and would like peace and quiet," Clancy told her over their cocktails. "Besides, I have something to tell you."

She looked quickly at his face. "It isn't bad news," she decided.

"No. It isn't. But evidently it will be news to you."

"Oh? I think I'll have the crab salad, Clancy."

"Soup?"

"Yes. Very hot."

He talked to the waiter, then turned back to her. Her hair was brushed and fastened, shining, back from her face. She wore a creamy tan shirt which might have been one of his own—tailored, well-fitting. "Did you get that shirt at Brooks Brothers?" he asked, his eyes smiling.

"As a matter of fact, I did. I often get blouses there. I like the cut and the tailoring."

He nodded. "Did you know," he asked, "that I had been elected to the hospital board?"

Gretchen gazed at him over the rim of her martini glass. Her eyes widened; he had surprised her. Completely.

And once she realized what he had said, she reacted in all directions at once. She choked a little on the drink and, sputtering, she set the glass down quickly and picked up the napkin. Her cheeks were red. "You *can't* be!" she cried. "What would you know about running a hospital? Whose daffy idea was this, anyway?"

Clancy watched her, listened, and waited.

"Why wasn't I told?" she asked finally, her tone a little harsh. She was very upset.

"I just did tell you."

"Yes, but—before— Nobody's said a word to me about it! When did this happen?"

"A week ago," he said quietly.

"But . . ."

"Perhaps the news came out in the newspaper. I'm pretty sure it's on the hospital's bulletin board. You could have seen it if you were there."

Now her face turned red all over, and her eyes blazed. "I am simply furious!" she cried, pounding her clenched fist on the table edge.

"I can see that you are," said Clancy.

"Did you say a week ago? And no one has said a word to me, before or afterward."

"Are you angry at me, Greta?" he asked softly.

"I'm as mad as hops about the whole thing! The sneaky way . . ."

"You're angry at me, too, aren't you?"

She looked at him in exasperation. "Oh, I never could be angry at you, Clancy! You stay so calm and reasonable. At least, I *shouldn't* be mad at you." She glanced up at his face. "Should I?"

"No," he said quietly. "No, you shouldn't."

The waiter brought their soup, clear, well-seasoned, and hot.

"I suppose," said Gretchen after a time, "they selected you because of the mobile unit."

One of his eyebrows went up. "That," he agreed, "or because they wanted a lawyer on their board."

"Mhmmmn. They thought this was a way to please me—everyone says I got the unit going."

"And you'd know just how responsible you were."

"I helped," she declared.

"Of course you did."

"As my husband . . ."

"As your husband, they thought I'd know how to handle doctors." He didn't look up at her.

"There's another thought," said Gretchen when her huge bowl of salad was brought. "We should divide this . . ."

"I ordered chops."

"Yes, I know. You always order lamb chops here."

"They know how to cook 'em. Well-done, but not hard. What's your other thought?"

"Oh. That the hospital is trying to get me to work."

Clancy made no comment.

"They should come right out and *ask* me," said Gretchen, again on the defensive.

"Hasn't Dr. Wagner asked you to go on staff?"

"Yes," said Gretchen, "he has."

"Why don't you? I've asked you to."

"I know. And I should do it, I suppose. It would mean long, regular hours. I'd need some help in the house . . ."

"You could get that help."

"I—" She laughed. "I simply cannot stand those three D.O.'s on the staff. And old Fielder."

Clancy laughed. "That's being pretty narrow-minded, isn't it?"

"You don't know what having to work with them means."

"No, I don't."

"Do you think I should go staff, Clancy?"

"So far as I am concerned, there's only one thing I'd rather see you do."

"Mhmmmn," said Gretchen. "Have a baby."

"That's right," he agreed. "Or two. Or three."

Clancy had debated about accepting the position on the hospital board. He tried to imagine how he would feel if Gretchen should take over some obligation in his field of work. Would he welcome a mutual interest? Was it better for each one to be separate? He had not expected her to be angry about the appointment, and he truly did not think she was angry at *him*. She knew that he was proud of her. When someone asked him, even tauntingly, what he thought of Gretchen's being president of the medical society, or about the mobile unit, he could say honestly and quickly that he was proud of his wife. But he did find that he was becoming more thoughtful about his replies to such questions.

Why should a figurehead doctor preside over the society? Was there more to Gretchen's connection with the mobile unit than having her picture taken, a beautiful smiling woman in white standing at the door of the red cross emblazoned trailer? She had had to hunt that bag of hers out of a box in the attic of her father's home.

He had told her that he would like to see her go on the hospital staff, and work at the job. If she did work at the hospital, there would need to be changes in their lives. They must hire someone to do the many household tasks which Gretchen now did, and they would be done with less flair and grace than she brought to those things. Gretchen would have obligations which would not let her, always, do the things Clancy enjoyed doing with her. Emergencies could arise, she would have to take her turn on call. But he still wished she would do it, go on staff, and work as that position would require. It could not be, would not be, all glamor. She could not get by with that alone.

Though he knew that she was accustomed to getting away with a great deal.

CHAPTER 6

WITHIN a month of their talk in the hotel dining room, Clancy came home from the office one late afternoon and found a strange woman scrubbing vegetables at the sink in Gretchen's pretty kitchen. He frowned. There were not many blacks in Idaho. He was sure he had seen this gray-uniformed woman before. . . .

"I am Mr. Cobbins," he said uncertainly. "Is my wife giving a party?"

"Not that I know, sir. I'm Vera. Vera Darrow. Miss Gretchen, she hire me to work for you folks."

"You— Haven't I seen you before?"

"Yes, sir. I been working for the Bennetts for fifteen years. Miss Kathy and Miss Gretchen, they grew up on my cookies and milk."

Clancy's lips pressed together.

"Why did you leave the Bennetts, Vera, and come here?"

"Miss Gretchen, she coax me. She said you thought she ought to have a cook-maid in this nice house."

"I see." So he was to blame. He had planted the idea

of household help—if Gretchen went on staff, that was. But she had not gone on staff.

"She sure got a cute way with her, Mr. Cobbins. She soft-talk me, an' I couldn't refuse her. She said so sorry-like that she wish she could have me work for you, she say that she couldn't doctor, an' take care of the house, an' feed a big, hungry man like you."

When had Gretchen started to "doctor"?

He took his briefcase back to the family room. "Where is Miss Gretchen?" he asked Vera.

"La, I don't know, sir. She skitin' around somewhere."

"I suppose. Well, Vera, I want you to go back to Mrs. Bennett. I'll drive you, and pay you for the work you've done here. But—"

"Mr. Cobbins, I can't do that! Miz Bennett won't let me. She tole me that. If I quit, she say, I could not come back! So if you don't let me stay here, I'm out of a job."

"That's nonsense," said Clancy. "Get your things. I'll talk to Mrs. Bennett."

The Bennett home was on the same street as the Pursers'. As Clancy drove into the Bennett property, Gretchen's car backed out of her father's drive. She must have seen him and Vera . . .

He thought she might come over. But she did not; he found her waiting at home, ready for a fight—a real fight, the nearest to a real one that they had ever come. That she had ever come. He sat silent, watched her, and let her talk. He knew that she could charm a bird from the trees and the long-established cook out of the kitchen of friends.

"I'd think you would be glad that someone like Vera

would come in . . ." she cried.

Clancy was not glad. He thought she would be better off taking care of her own home or doing hospital work. Or having a family.

He didn't need to tell her these things. "We like to entertain," she cried, facing him, very beautiful in her anger and her excitement. Her bright skirt swirled about her knees, her eyes flashed. "Don't you enjoy the amusing parties we can give? You know darn well they are good for your business!"

They were amusing parties, and he did enjoy them. The house filled with their friends, laughing, talking, drinking and eating. Sangria and tacos. Hot buttered rum and tiny sausages on toothpicks. Gretchen always hired a man to attend to passing the trays of drinks; their yardman helped clean up the next day. Clancy did enjoy the parties—they always ended in the kitchen, with a huge coffee urn bubbling and Gretchen scrambling eggs in a pan big enough to use for sliding downhill in the snow.

He waited.

And, finally, Gretchen, disheveled, flushed, came to sit on the bright, shaggy carpet, put her hand on his knee and looked up at him.

"How can I fight you, Clancy," she asked, "if you won't fight back?"

He cupped her face in his hands, leaned forward and kissed her. "We don't need to fight, Gretchen."

"You made a fool of me with the Bennetts."

"I don't think so. They know you, maybe better than I do. And you knew, before you talked to Vera, how I would feel."

"You said . . ."

"We both know what was said. Here, sit up here with me."

He held her close, and she lay soft in his arms.

"Isn't this what you want, Clancy?" she asked after a time.

"You know the things I want, Gretchen. Right now, supper. But to take the long view . . ."

She got to her feet. "Let me guess," she cried. "For me to go on staff. And have a family . . ."

"That's right," Clancy agreed. "And go on giving your delightful parties, however you've been managing this past year or two."

He stood up and drew her close again. "Shouldn't we be planning that first child, Greta?" he asked.

"I don't know. I'm planning on a rock garden for this next summer. Our lawn looks terrible."

"We've been sprigging hardy grass. Once it takes hold . . ."

She moved toward the kitchen and Vera's abandoned vegetables. "I have an idea," she said. "Suppose we don't have any grass. Just the trees, and plantings, and small stretches of pebbles . . ."

Clancy went back to his chair and the newspaper; she would come around. He should wait and watch. Twenty-seven years of having her own way needed to be overbalanced. He loved her, she loved him. And she would come around.

During that summer, the town, their friends, talked about Gretchen's "rock garden." It was a crazy idea, but it seemed to be working. Their home took on a certain

Oriental look. "And no grass to cut!" the men pointed out.

"But weeds to pull, and careful watering of the shrubbery, the fruit trees, and the evergreens."

People, their friends, were watching the young Cobbinses. Til Holt and Kathy had made quite a story of the theft of Vera and her return. Sometimes they even teased Gretchen or Clancy about that.

Mrs. Purser heard about it and asked her husband what they should do. "Nothing," said Hugh. "Clancy's done it. We spoiled the girl, Mary. I am glad she was lucky enough to get a husband to go on with that."

"He is very fond of Gretchen."

"So were we. But we were soft, too."

By the time Gretchen's "rock garden" was well under way—and showing that it would work—the many-toned shrubs and trees made patterns as lovely as any flowers. The flowering bushes were just right, or were dug up and planted elsewhere.

"Gretchen's worked like a Trojan in that yard," said Hugh Purser admiringly.

"She's a strong, healthy girl," said her mother.

"Is she still working with the mobile unit?"

"I certainly hope so." He would check, and was not too surprised to find that she did, occasionally, fail to take her turn.

This disappointed him, and for the first time since her marriage he protested with his daughter. "You seemed to be doing such a fine job there, Gretchen," he said.

"It's working all right. I'm no great shakes as a doctor, Dad."

"You could be if you would stick with it. When you

graduated, your teachers told me that you had great promise."

"But they thought I should do an internship."

He smiled. "That was mentioned, yes. I didn't argue because I was happy to have you come home. Wagner had told me that they could use you at the hospital."

"I work there."

"As a volunteer," said Clancy, coming in on the conversation.

"Now, Clancy . . ." said Gretchen warningly.

Clancy carefully arranged the bright green soaker around a clump of yews, and turned on the water. "Gretchen," he told his father-in-law, coming back to sit on the edge of the deck, "gets the idea for her rock garden, and then makes me work at the thing."

"I'm afraid that's how she does everything," said Hugh Purser. "I was just rebuking her for not working regularly at the mobile unit."

Clancy turned his head to look at Gretchen, who was stretched out on a long chair, a pair of sunglasses concealing her eyes. "Aren't you?" he asked.

"We all miss occasionally," she murmured.

"But why should *you* miss?"

She lifted the glasses enough to look at her father. "He thinks I have nothing else to do," she explained. "I keep house, I work at the hospital—and little old Dr. Shaw is always ready and willing to take my turn."

"Do the patients like him as much?"

Gretchen said nothing.

"You object to the D.O.'s working with the M.D.'s," Clancy pointed out, "then you give this man a chance to take an M.D.'s place."

"Oh, Clancy!"

"I mean what I say, Greta, and I have your father as a witness. I've no doubt that Shaw or one of the other younger men is willing to substitute, but I want you to stop asking them. You're to take your turn with the unit, and work at that job."

Hugh Purser's one eye was bright to see what response Gretchen would make to that order.

He expected fireworks, but all she said was a plaintive "Don't fight with me, Clancy."

"No," he agreed, "I won't fight with you. But you're to do this job, my dear, and you're to do it right."

She turned her head, so she must be looking at her husband.

"Let's ride the canal," she said unexpectedly.

Clancy laughed and went into the house to answer the telephone.

"Do you two ever ride the canal?" Hugh asked his daughter.

They were referring to the local practice of launching a rubber raft or a large tire into the swift waters of the gravity irrigation canal, and letting themselves be carried through the city, through culverts and under bridges, dodging the overhanging tree branches and other riders. Teen-agers were the bold ones, usually, and often there were accidents, even disasters.

"I used to do it," Gretchen told her father. "I'd love to get Clancy to do it just once."

"He won't, Gretchen. He's too sensible a man."

She sat up and swept the glasses away. "And he always gets his way!" she cried. "People say I'm stubborn and spoiled. But I can promise you, Dad, that I am not a *patch* on that Cobbins fellow! He—" She looked up at Clancy, who had come out of the house. He had changed to a light blue pullover and dark blue slacks.

"Will you mind the hose, Greta?" he asked. "I have to go out."

"For how long?"

"I don't know. You could go home with your dad and spend the evening with your folks."

"Just like that . . ." murmured Gretchen as they watched Clancy get into his car and drive away.

"It must have been important, dear."

She tossed her hair back from her face. "Oh, it's always *important!* Not that he'll tell me what this emergency was. He never tells me a thing. But do you know—often as not his client with a so-called emergency is a cute little dark-haired woman named Susan Warrington. And your guess is as good as mine if he goes on business or for pleasure!"

"Gretchen, my dear . . ."

She stepped down from the deck. "I'll go move the hose," she said crossly. "Why don't you go home and get Mom, and we'll eat supper here. There's just a thin chance that Clancy will get back by ten or eleven."

"He'll know where you are."

Gretchen only sniffed and went on to move the hose. Her father followed her. He was wondering if he should worry about this young couple.

"Did you know they had fights?" he asked his wife when he was bringing her back for Gretchen's supper of fruit salad and toasted cheese sandwiches.

"I think Clancy is in love with her."

"He tries to make her do things she doesn't want to do."

"Yes. And usually he does make her. I wish he'd make her have a baby."

"Not until she wants to. She'd not make a very good mother if she was against the idea."

Clancy came home a little after eight. The sky was ablaze with pre-sunset color. He kissed Mary Purser, told Gretchen that, sure, he was hungry. One sandwich would do to start. Could they have some of that thin-sliced ham?

"If you'll slice it thin," said Gretchen, accepting his kiss.

He ate his supper, the dishes were put into the machine with the ones from the earlier meal. They were all sitting out on the deck again, in the half-dark, with sweaters and brandy—

"Quite a something happened down in town," said Clancy unexpectedly.

Gretchen's head went up.

"That call I had this afternoon," said Clancy, "was from Susan Warrington."

"A-huh!" said Gretchen.

Clancy laughed. "This time it was. You know," he explained to Hugh Purser, "Gretchen tries very hard to make poor Sue into the other woman in my life."

"Oh, no, Clancy," protested Mrs. Purser. "She's older than you are!"

Gretchen laughed; they all laughed. "I don't think she is, Mother," said Gretchen. "Not enough to ensure a thing."

"Can you tell us what was wrong, Clancy?" asked Hugh.

"Yes. Sure. It will be in the paper. A police case . . ."

Now everyone gasped. What on earth . . . ? Had Sue been hurt?

"Tell us!" said Gretchen firmly.

"I'm going to. Given a chance."

"Give him his chance," Gretchen told her parents. "These times don't come around very often."

"When we've been married fifty years," Clancy pointed out, "Gretch may just have learned about professional immunity."

"We'll not be here then," said Mary.

"I know about it now," Gretchen assured her. "But let's hear what Clancy can tell us. All right, Big Boy—"

"There had been a robbery," said Clancy. "She wanted the household inventory to be able to tell what was missing. I had to get that out of my files, then go to the house . . ."

"Tell us about the robbery!" Gretchen insisted. "How, when— In her house?"

"It was in her house," said Clancy. "She and the Int-Velds had taken their camper up to Lucky Peak Friday afternoon. Left about five."

"They asked us to go," Gretchen reminded him.

"I know they did. I couldn't take so much time. But Sue went with them. They left about five. They came home—oh, about an hour before she called me here." He glanced at Gretchen.

"You didn't say it was Sue," she told him, "but I suspected it was."

"What had happened?" asked Hugh.

"Someone had thrown a large rock—a very large one

—through a window at the back of the house. My word! You never saw so much glass! In splinters, all over the place. The whole house was in something of a mess. They'd opened drawers, spilled things out—"

"What was taken?"

"Evidently the burglar, or burglars, were hunting money. But they took some liquor and drank some on the spot. Searched the bedrooms, pulled mattresses off the beds—stole a diamond pin and a ring—and a fur coat."

"Her white beaver?" cried Gretchen.

"Yes. But left behind a newer mink jacket. Didn't touch it. Oh, I have a list of things missing or destroyed."

"Did they find money?"

"Less than fifty dollars. She keeps some money in a couple of places for change, cash payments to the boy who cuts her grass, taxi fare for her maid—things of that nature."

"I do the same thing," said Gretchen. "Just to be sure I have cash."

"And your cleaning woman probably knows where you keep it."

"Oh, sure. Do you think . . ." She stiffened and turned to Clancy. "Do suppose that fellow who bothered her a while ago—who said his name was Warrington—do you suppose that he . . . ?"

Clancy put his coffee cup down on its saucer; he picked up his brandy glass. And he looked sternly at his wife. "Now listen to me," he said firmly. "I don't want any of you three, and especially not Gretchen, speculating about who did this. We don't know who did it . . ."

"It could have been someone who saw them up at the lake," said Mary Purser.

"Weren't there clues, Clancy?" asked Hugh.

"There may have been. I'm leaving that to the police. My point is, because of my connection with the case, if you speculate, and someone hears you, that someone could jump to the conclusion that you are repeating things I had said."

"They don't know you," said Gretchen dryly. "But mind what the man says, Mom and Dad. I only hope he stands ready to protect me as fiercely as he does his precious professional integrity."

Clancy laughed.

Hugh said he was sure that Gretchen understood about such things.

Mary said she was sure that Clancy would give Gretchen any protection she might ever need.

Clancy smiled at her. "And don't talk about this," he repeated.

Gretchen did not. And she had no thought that her mother had talked. Though the next day . . .

She had gone to the hospital "to help out."

"Because I felt guilty about the things Dad and Clancy had said on Sunday evening," she told herself. She was not ready to make that sort of admission to anyone else.

There were always things she could do at the hospital. Take charge in the emergency room, take histories for new admissions, and, on this morning, help with an inventory of the drug room. While she was busy at this, Dr. Wagner came to the door and asked if she would telephone around town and find out if a certain rarely used drug would be available.

"If you can't locate it here, call Salt Lake, or even Denver, and have them ship it up on the evening plane."

"Yes, Dr. Wagner," said Dr. Cobbins. "What do you use it for?"

"Poison ivy."

"Poison . . ." She turned to look at him. "Where do people get poison ivy out here in the desert?"

"I don't know. Maybe they brought it with them when they set out to tour the beautiful northwest."

"I thought calamine . . ."

"Doesn't work. Nothing works in this case. I've put the patient to bed. I think this sulfa preparation might help."

"With shots."

"I've given the shots, Doctor. And if you don't think extra measures are called for, don't you ever acquire a fulminating case of poison ivy."

"I'll try not to," laughed Gretchen. She reached for the telephone.

She was calling the second pharmacy. The clerk answered and said, "Oh, hello, Dr. Cobbins, how are you this beautiful morning? And what can I do for you?" when another voice broke in on the line. The voice of an old person, eager, but trembling as well.

"Gretchen, is that you?"

"Wait a minute!" said Gretchen.

"Hang up that extension!" said the pharmacist.

"I just want to ask you one thing!" said the quavering and determined voice. "I'm here at the store. I am a good customer. I heard the druggist speaking to you, Gretchen—"

"What is it you want, Mrs. Callier?" asked Gretchen coldly. She could picture the old lady; she must have tottered behind the cashier's desk and taken the phone from the shelf. Somewhere close would be Marcella, holding the walker. But Ida B. had the telephone. It was a warm, sunny morning, but the old lady would have a fur stole, at least, around her shoulders. A small hat would rest on her lavender curls, and—

"Tell me quickly," said Gretchen firmly. Talking to Ida B. would be the quickest way to speak to the pharmacist.

"I know you're busy," said Mrs. Callier, "but I did want to ask you about Sue Warrington."

"What about her?" asked Gretchen icily.

"I heard she'd had a robber at her house. Was she hurt?"

"I couldn't say, Mrs. Callier. Would you please . . . ?"

"Was it that fellow who tried to move in on Susan?"

Gretchen made no reply.

"Did they get much?" Mrs. Callier swept on. "I'm sure Clancy knows all about it."

"So?" said Gretchen.

"Now, my dear, don't be rude. I thought . . ."

"It will all be in the paper, Mrs. Callier. Now will you please get off the phone? I have something important—" She broke off. If she told she was at the hospital and was making an emergency call to the pharmacy, the bloodhounds would really be baying! She hung up. After five minutes she would again try to talk to that pharmacist.

That evening, when Clancy came home, she was still furious.

"What's wrong with you?" he asked. "And why aren't you dressed? Aren't we due at Jim Adams's party?"

"We're not going," said Gretchen.

"What do you mean we're not going? Engraved invitations, we accepted— Of course we are going!"

"And find our place cards next to, or across from, Ida B.?" she asked.

"Now, Greta . . ."

"We do, whenever we attend a big party. People think they have to ask her because they accept *her* invitations, which she passes out only so she'll be invited to *these* bashes. And not knowing where to seat her, they inflict her on me. Because I've known her all her life—"

"She's known you all your life," Clancy corrected.

"I've decided that that is going to stop. I may not go to any party for a year. Just to break the pattern."

"What's got into you? I know Ida B. and her niece are bores, but—Jim's our friend. Of course we're going to this dinner for his parents' anniversary. What's happened to you, anyway?"

He took her arm and guided her to the bedroom. "Do you need to shower?" he asked.

"I showered when I came home from the hospital."

"All right. Get out your dress and your slippers while I shower, and you can tell me while we're dressing."

She did tell him. Dressed in her long white silk jersey with its sash of vivid green, she still was saying that she would not expose herself to the Callier women. Arrived at the country club, she went straight to the dining room and examined the place cards. She came back waving her own. "May I change my card?" she asked her hostess, Dora Dell Adams.

"Well, I suppose so, Gretchen. Where do you want to sit?"

"I don't care. And I'll find a place."

"I thought husbands and wives need not sit together . . ." said her hostess.

"Let her alone," said Clancy. "She's mad at Mrs. Callier."

"Oh, dear. And her card was right next to Gretch's. The old lady is so fond of her."

"Not any more, I'm afraid," said Clancy darkly, going after his wife. He couldn't tell why the girl was mad, but he was ready to help her find a neighbor for Ida B.

She found one. It was Susan Warrington, and Clancy switched that card for his own. "I should never forgive you," he told his laughing wife as they drove home. "Though I see now what you mean by being stuck with your friend Ida B."

"We should not go to parties if . . ."

"If we have to sit with her. You're right. Let's stay home for a year."

"That's what I told you hours ago."

"Did you know she has alabaster skin?" asked Clancy.

"And washes it with Palmolive soap," laughed his wife. "Oh, Clancy, Clancy, why don't you ever let me tell you things!"

"I may, from now on," said her husband. "You seemed to be having a ball this evening."

"I did. We had a great table. Kathy got tiddly, of course. And Til Holt was in great form."

"Hmmmn," said Clancy.

CHAPTER 7

FOR YEARS afterward, Gretchen was to look back on that summer, and the autumn which followed, as being incredibly long and full. "I can't really sort things out," she would say thoughtfully.

There was the Jim Adams party—where she had played musical chairs with poor Clancy—she had worn her white jersey and Dolly IntVeld had looked beautiful in mauve. Kathy had drunk too much; her friends were beginning to worry about her drinking—and Til Holt told her off in no uncertain terms. And she had told Til that he needn't worry any more; she was going to stop trying to marry him. "All you do is scold me."

And Gretchen had talked to Dr. Wagner about going on staff.

"Clancy keeps after me to do it," she said. "He doesn't realize that the hospital might not want a know-nothing like me. And I'm pretty sure they are right."

"Do you want to come here on that sort of basis, Gretchen?" asked Dr. Wagner.

"I don't know what I want. I'd like to please Clancy

and my parents. But I, myself—"

"You're afraid to commit yourself as an M.D."

Her eyes flew wide. "How did you know that?"

He shrugged. "Everybody has fears of taking a significant step in his life. The first kiss, marriage— You wanted to be a doctor enough to go through the grind of medical school, but when it came to taking authority, away from your teachers . . ."

"You've known this all along?"

"Of course."

"All right. Could I learn to be a doctor?"

"No. You've done the studying. Now the question is, could you *be* a doctor?"

"I suppose."

"I'll present your name to the Board."

"I hope Clancy won't vote against me."

"Nobody will vote against you."

The next week, she went on staff. As her first assignment, she took duty in Intensive Care.

"I'm scared to death," she confessed to Dr. Wagner.

"Don't be. You know the things you need to know."

At the end of the next week, she served as bridesmaid for Kathy Bennett when she married Barney Binnard, a rancher who was making money fast with his hop fields. No one knew Barney very well.

Her friends thought Kathy was paying Til Holt off for not asking her to marry him. Til knew they said this.

"If she would stop drinking . . ." he tried to explain to Gretchen and Clancy.

"Binnard himself has a problem," Gretchen agreed.

"She says she is going to live in that farmhouse."

"With long visits to her parents."

No one was happy about the marriage. But what could one do?

And before the next month was out, the deepest sort of tragedy struck the hospital. Gretchen still was serving the Intensive Care Unit five days a week; Dr. Fielder and Dr. Giamonco were the others on that service. She was gaining confidence. "If I can't do the job as well as that old man and—and—"

Clancy put his hand over her mouth.

She shrugged away. "I am getting better about that, too," she told him. "I don't even want to specify them so often."

"Isn't their work adequate, Gretchen?"

"I'm not really a judge, Clancy. They seem a little eager to work, to please. They talk medicine in big, big words. They want every test for every case, and, I think, they are somewhat knife-happy."

"Dr. Wagner—"

"So long as he is surgical chief, they are restrained. Yes. Dr. Tipton takes care of the medical side. But, Clancy . . ."

"I think it is a problem most hospitals share, Gretchen. With Federal money financing the institution, the medical examinations and licensure cannot exclude these doctors. They are building and filling new medical schools all the time."

"And they are just as good as M.D.'s," she said gloomily. "You've noticed that no one ever says we're as good as they are?"

"I think it helps for all M.D.'s, including my beautiful wife, to be at work."

"Even if you have to eat TV dinners five nights a week?"

He laughed. "I don't remember eating one."

"When you do, you can accept Mother's offer to feed you."

"I'll do that."

So Gretchen worked, and became accustomed to working. She brushed up on her medical books in her free time, and bought new, well-fitting lab coats and jackets. She knew that she was still leaning heavily on Dr. Wagner for advice and encouragement, but since it was always there, she did not worry about herself too much.

And then, without any warning, without any chance to plan for the emergency, Dr. Wagner was stricken with a massive brain hemorrhage, lay like a log of wood for two days, and then mercifully died.

Mercifully for him. The loss was a great tragedy to the hospital staff, and to Gretchen.

"What will I *do?*" she asked Clancy pitiably.

"Whatever all of us must do. His wife, the Board, the other doctors and the patients. We all must find ways to continue his work, to carry it on."

"I can't, without him."

"Yes, you can. Tipton will take over."

"He's not Dr. Wagner. He doesn't understand my situation."

"You may not have any great situation, Gretchen."

She looked at him in amazement. "You know I do!" she challenged.

"Lack of experience. You can surely remind Tipton of that."

"I'll try."

And she did try. Just as she did miss Dr. Wagner, whom she had heard one patient describe as "a very normal, a very warm man."

At first these terms had outraged her as inadequate. Then she came to acknowledge them as fitting. There had never been any fireworks about Dr. Wagner. He went quietly, normally, about his work, and his warmth did as much for his patients as did his skilled hands.

Dr. Tipton—

An internist, he was a very good doctor, more volatile than Biron Wagner, more quick to make judgments. In his early forties, he was ready to work long hours, but he wanted to be free to study, to attend symposiums and seminars.

He liked Gretchen, but she felt his was not as deep an understanding as had been Dr. Wagner's.

"Do the work assigned you," he prescribed. "I'll tell you if you make mistakes."

Which seemed to be working out fairly well. Except that, very soon after Dr. Wagner's death, Carl Tipton told the Board that he was leaving the hospital.

"I've been planning this," he said. "I knew that I wanted to learn and to work under other circumstances. Wagner's sudden death showed me that I must get about the life I want to have."

"Did you know about this?" Clancy asked Gretchen.

She was too shocked to speak. She could only shake her head.

"He has acknowledged that he knows he is leaving the hospital and the town short," said Clancy.

"It finishes me," said Gretchen.

"Now, Greta . . ."

"But it does, Clancy! I think the hospital might as well shut down."

"Where would your patients go?"

"Who's going to be Chief of Staff? A young D.O.? Or Dr. Fielder?"

"We're going to find someone. Meanwhile . . ."

"You don't understand, Clancy—"

"I know I don't. But I'm going to keep on trying."

"And you want me to do the same thing."

"Our decision on a new doctor or two can be as vital as your service. You've been trained. You've learned a lot these past few months under Wagner and Tipton. I am not asking you to take charge, Greta. Just to stay in there and try to help the sick people. If you can't, send them elsewhere. But *be* there. The Board wants you to do that!"

Medical school graduates opened offices without internships. Gretchen wished she had that sort of courage. She would need it. But she still felt helpless when the people of the town—not Clancy, or her parents, or her friends—just the townspeople appeared to count on her; they had called on her to help them at the hospital when they were sick or hurt.

People would call her at home—the man who delivered their mail called her, identified himself, and said his son—ten years old—had a high fever and pain in his side. "You're the only doctor I know . . ."

Of course she must tell him that she would meet him at the hospital. The boy had an inflamed appendix. Yes, she would stay with him, but she was not a surgeon, and she could not operate. The case was hers, and the boy did well. The parents were grateful and spread the word.

A complete stranger heard that word and approached her on the street. "My mother is old; I think she is dying. Could I bring her to the hospital? Would you examine her and tell me what to do? A nursing home, or maybe —something—"

And then, springing the trap entirely shut, there was Dolly IntVeld, Gretchen's dear friend.

Gretchen knew that Dolly had essential hypertension; she knew what Dr. Tipton had done for her in the way of medication and advice. When, one night, Dolly collapsed in the bathroom of their home, and Jonah called first the ambulance and then Gretchen—at three in the morning—

"Please stay with her, Gretch," he begged tearfully. "I'm sure it's a stroke."

"Jonah, I'm not qualified . . ."

"You know enough to tell me if the other doctors are doing the right thing for her. I can trust you. She is so precious to me, Gretchen."

She was precious to Gretchen, too. "If I had gone to work right after I got my M.D.," she told Clancy as she hurriedly dressed to go to the hospital, "I'd know enough now to help Dolly."

"Maybe you would," said Clancy, dressing, too. "But as of now you can certainly help Jonah."

Yes, she could. "Where are you going?"

"To drive you, and then to hold Jonah's hand."

One of the osteopaths on the staff, and Dr. Fielder, said that there probably was a brain aneurysm. Surgery was the only hope. It would be too risky to move Dolly to Portland or to Salt Lake City. It was risky to wait. But a surgeon was flown in.

Gretchen stood by helplessly. And though all their friends were holding prayer hours in the different homes, Gretchen could not pray. Dolly, her shaven head a beehive of bandages, survived the surgery, wakened to recognize Jonah and Gretchen, then died an hour after Jonah had left the hospital.

This completely shocked Gretchen, and Clancy found it difficult to know what to do or say to her. He begged her not to give up her hospital work as she vowed she would do. But he himself was badly shaken.

He did manage to find and hire a couple to take care of their house—a man about thirty-five and his younger wife, who was a deaf-mute, but an excellent cook. They took good care of the Cobbins property, and Gretchen found herself learning the sign language so that she could communicate with Delmo Lorella. This pleased Stephen, the husband. "We lose jobs because my woman makes people nervous," he said.

"How stupid," said Gretchen.

"Though if I don't stay at the hospital," she said to Clancy, "I won't need them."

"You're going to stay. They need you there."

"A fat lot I do."

"With your mind at ease about the TV dinners, you'll relax and do better."

Gretchen laughed. "And you like the way Stephen trims the firs, too," she said. "And Delmo's cornsticks."

Clancy stretched out on the long chair. "I certainly do. So . . . ?"

"I'm still going to the hospital every day," she reminded him.

"Do I dare tell you . . ." he began, then shook his head. "No, I don't."

"Tell me what?"

"I don't want you mad, though a different target might help."

"Clancy . . ."

"All right, all right. I'll tell you. Or do you know that the night after Dolly was buried, and the relatives had all gone home, Mrs. Callier invited Jonah to dinner?"

Gretchen frowned. "Why? Didn't she know the poor man . . . ?"

"Your mother asked her why. And she said two things. That Jonah was now a most eligible man, with his beautiful home and all. And Marcella was a fine woman. Ida B. had to look out for her interest."

Gretchen stared at Clancy. "She—she—Clancy Cobbins, I *hate* people!"

"Oh, no, you don't."

"Yes, I do. And that's no state of mind for a doctor."

"So get rid of the state of mind. Because—"

She put up her hand. "Saying I'm a doctor doesn't make me one."

That time, Clancy could not find anything to say to her. He feared that the problem had taken them beyond his depth.

Though the next afternoon, something was said and done for him. He himself was not to know of the event. It affected Gretchen, but she did not realize how important it was at the particular time, and she did not tell Clancy about the little incident.

On duty in ICU from seven until three, she had formerly needed to get home and care for her house and Clancy.

But with the blessed Lorellas there to have the house clean and opened, dinner cooking in the oven when Clancy came home, Gretchen could give a little time to her own interests. She could shop for some skirts and sweaters. She could do the marketing and buy a roast for the weekend. She could go to the beauty parlor.

"I need the works," she told the operator. "I've been biting my nails and washing my hair myself when I take a shower."

She had been properly shampooed, and was under the dryer, ready for a manicure, when the telephone rang. She and the operator both listened.

"Mrs. Keen doesn't come in till five," said the girl at the desk.

Mrs. Keen was one of the two nurse-anesthetists at the hospital, and not one of Gretchen's favorite people.

"But I'm not one of hers, probably," she often reminded herself.

"Should I have her call the hospital when she comes in?" the desk girl was asking. "All right. Thank you."

"Must be an emergency," she told anyone interested. "She said she hopes to find Keen before then."

"Will you be needed?" Gretchen's operator asked her, speaking softly.

"I doubt it. I'm not on emergency call."

"Good. I want to soak your nails in hot oil."

Gretchen was still at the manicure table when Mrs. Keen blew into the shop. She was a tall, big-boned woman who moved rapidly and spoke loudly. The desk girl told her of the call from the hospital, and she barely swallowed a sizzling phrase of annoyance. But she did pick up the telephone and dialed it.

"Keen here," she said, her voice and her eyes angry.

"Did you call me?" She listened. "When?" she snapped.

She turned to Gretchen's operator. "Can I come back at five-thirty?" she asked.

She was told that she could. She slammed down the phone and that time made no effort to swallow her comment as she departed, banging the shop door behind her.

Gretchen sat thoughtful. The time involved suggested that probably there had been an accident with a broken bone needing to be set and cast.

"She doesn't give a damn about the poor patient," said the young woman who was putting polish on Gretchen's nails. "If I ever need surgery, I hope my anesthetist would not be her."

Gretchen was surprised. "I thought you two were friends."

"In a way, we are, yes. But still— She's trained, she's needed. But she could be human, too."

Again Gretchen sat thoughtful. Just twenty-four hours before, when she had protested to Jonah IntVeld about Ida B.'s performance, and she had said, "That woman needs to be told a thing or two!"

Jonah had touched her hand. "Don't you be the one to tell her, Gretch. I believe I can take care of myself."

Now—knowing that Clancy had run out of things to say to her, to persuade her to stay on at the hospital, she would try saying, at least to herself, "I believe I can take care of myself." He would be glad if she did.

The next day, early in the morning, with the skylight showing the dawn sky streaked with pink, the pines and firs on the mountainside awakening to the first rays of the sun, Gretchen touched Clancy's shoulder. He stirred but did not waken, and she smiled to herself. She watched the shadows draw into the corners of the bedroom. Gretchen's room. Clancy always called it that when their house was being shown to someone.

It was her room. A charming French provincial room with the proper French furniture for it. On the walls was a French striped paper of soft blue and dusty pink. At the windows were white, full-length, embroidered, tambour curtains. Doorknobs were flower-painted, as were the accessories of the adjoining bathroom. A Wedgwood blue carpet was underfoot and the skylight over their heads with, that morning, the sky matching the colors of their room. Gretchen smiled softly and glanced again at her husband, surprised to find his eyes open and watchful.

"You've been watching me!" she accused.

He lifted on one elbow to kiss her. "Wondering what canary you had just eaten," he said.

She laughed softly. "I was enjoying the sunrise."

"Comes too damn early this far north."

"And admiring our bedroom."

"*That's* the canary!"

"Well, maybe. Though I may be about to eat another one."

"Gretchen . . ."

"Don't worry. It's just—I've been thinking."

"Oh, oh!"

"I think a lot about Dolly these days, Clancy."

"Yes, we all do."

"And what Jonah said about being able to take care of himself."

"He can. He's a strong man."

"I envy him. But I do wish I could have helped Dolly."

"Gretchen . . ."

"I know, I know. But I have made up my mind, and it hasn't been easy under the circumstances, Clancy. And of course it is way too late to do Dolly any good. But I wanted you to know that I've decided to stay on floor duty at the hospital, to work as I can until I learn the things I need to know."

He put his arm under her shoulders and drew her close. "You know what this means?"

"Of course I know. Taking orders from Shaw and Giamonco. And Fielder. Doing their scut work—"

"You could go to some other hospital."

"And leave you? Anyway, what proof do you have that they would be better?"

"None," he admitted. "And I'd hate like hell to have you gone."

"Okay, then. I'll get the training and experience bit over with. And keep an eye on you while I'm doing it. Now you take another forty winks while I shower and dress." She rolled out of bed and was halfway across the room before he could protest. He lay listening, half-smiling, watching her as she moved in and out of the big room.

Gretchen. As he had first seen her and fallen in love with her. As she was that morning. Her slim body seemed always to be at perfect ease; feeling stirred within her like smoke rising in warm air. Her skin was the color of ripe apricots, her lips were full and soft. She was a strong young woman, and in any project at hand —a ski trip, planting her rock garden, now this project of doctoring—she was ready to work, not showing distaste for any of the tasks involved.

If Gretchen did this, if she stayed with it . . .

"Hey, Gretch!" he cried, getting out of bed himself. "You know what? I'm proud of you!"

Not admiring the other four staff doctors, not even respecting them as doctors, she would, she announced, remain on the staff and do what she could. Yes, she would assist each one as needed; yes, she would take her turn on call. It would be house duty, since she had no office or patients of her own.

It was not a good setup, but it would suffice until things changed—for the better, she hoped. She did not mention the word "intern" to these men, nor did they to her.

But the doctors all watched her from day to day. They all knew that Shaw still resented her position on who should have done the surgery on Dolly IntVeld. They suspected that she still felt a D.O.'s training was not equal to that of an M.D. But they would watch and see how things worked . . .

Gretchen followed the same course. She did what she was told or asked to do, she worked closely with Dr. Shaw, and found time for a heavy course of reading, both in current journals and among the books in Dr. Wagner's library, which still filled the shelves of his empty office. She did what she was told and voiced her opinions only when asked.

She kept her own file of cases that seemed particular; sometimes she talked about these to Clancy, who was a good listener. She said from the first that she did not expect advice from him. "I couldn't use it. These men . . ."

"Are they totally incompetent, Greta?"

"No, they're not. It's just—occasionally—well, take a case we had yesterday. This patient was brought in—a man injured in a farm accident. We were thirty-five miles away. I was assigned to receive him and work him up. That means examine, get a history, observe—

"This man . . ." She sat silent. "When he came in, his hand was limp, even icy. At first there was not even the faint flutter of a pulse. And then, after a second or two, I could pick one up, but racing crazily. Then it went away—and came back. His limbs were rigid. I decided it was shock, of course. And I wrote down that it appeared to be a classic example of internal hemorrhaging. Shaw didn't like that *classic.*"

"How do you get along with Shaw?"

She shrugged. "All right. Now that he's found that he can't make a pass at me and—"

"*What?*" Clancy was up out of his chair.

She laughed and reached for his hand. "Relax," she said. "He's the kind that has to make a pass at a woman if he sees her close at hand."

"Because . . ."

"No, no! Not because he is an osteopath, darling Board member. And I can handle what he is."

"He thinks he should be Chief of Staff."

"If he or any of those four becomes Chief, my medical career will be at an end."

He sat down again. "I don't like it."

She said nothing.

"How did your *classic* case turn out?" he asked.

"Oh, he died, of course. I wanted an autopsy, but Shaw won't do 'em."

"Isn't he supposed to?"

"I don't know what he is supposed to do, Clancy. *I* suppose you could find out."

"Wagner did them?"

"Yes, he did. Of course. But here again, this may be a personal thing with Shaw. They could have brought a pathologist in. We send tissue samples and smears to a commercial lab all the time."

"Aren't we equipped . . . ?"

"Not in man power. It's very hard to get and keep personnel under our peculiar circumstances."

"Not having a Chief of Staff?"

"That's a large part of it."

"But not all. Hmmmn."

There were times and situations when Gretchen thought that the hospital doctors should talk to a lawyer. She wanted to remind them that they had one on the Board. But since that one was Clancy—

"Tell me what we should be doing," she asked that attorney as they waited one evening for Stephen Lorella to summon them to dinner.

"By 'we' you mean . . . ?"

"The doctors at the hospital. I don't want to argue with them, Clancy, unless I am sure of my grounds. I've done some reading, I try to remember the short course in forensic medicine which I had in med school . . ."

He looked at her sharply. "What on earth is going on down there?" he asked.

"Nothing. And nothing may go on. But I would like your legal opinion."

"My fee . . ."

"Send the bill to my husband. Seriously, Clancy—"

"Oh, dear. Well, all right. What is it?"

"A matter of a transfusion for a patient who is dying and doesn't want a transfusion."

"Will one save his life?"

"Prolong it, probably. For a time."

"What does the family say?"

"That's the point. He has no close family. No wife or dependent children such as the books talk about."

"Is he lucid?"

"Yes, he is. But some of the men want to get a court order for the transfusion."

"Which the old man does not want."

"That's right."

"Don't worry about it. I don't think they could get such a court order. The ruling is pretty well-established that the individual who is the subject of the medical decision has the final say."

"Should I try to tell Fielder and Giamonco that?"

"Not as coming from me. They probably won't go to court. If they'd ask me, I'd tell them."

"I see. Could I sort of whisper that you are on the Board and available for advice?"

"A whisper maybe. Don't worry about it."

"I'm not worrying. I am trying to learn. There are cases, aren't there? For forced transfusions?"

"Well, it's always tricky, Gretchen. It's not a matter of suicide, or a man's right to take his life; it's rather a matter of his refusing life-saving methods."

"And some religions . . ."

"They are not without limits, Greta. We can't interfere with a man's religious beliefs. But we can, on occasion, interfere with his religious practices."

"Rattlesnakes."

Clancy chuckled. "Yes, and refused transfusions. Say—let me think—say you have the dying mother of an infant. She refuses therapeutic, even life-saving transfusions. The court could call that an act of irresponsibility, and order it done. Because, you see, the state will not allow the abandonment of a child, and this ultimate abandonment would be construed . . ."

"You're smart," said Gretchen. "I read that a transfusion could be ordered for a delirious or irrational patient."

"To save his life, yes. It's stronger if a family asks for it, but the hospital or doctor can step in and protect the patient against his own helplessness. However, your old man . . ."

"I know. Thank you, darling. You're handier to have around than any thick old book."

"I have my good features. And my fee . . ."

"That's all taken care of. I told Delmo to cook an extra pork chop for you."

"And I'll eat it and gain five pounds from a half-pound chop!"

Sometimes, not often, she would call him at the office. "Could I speak to Mr. Cobbins? This is Mrs. Cobbins. Yes, it is important."

Clancy would come on. "What is it, Greta?"

"And you're busy. All right. Clancy, what about baby sitters?"

"What about 'em? Are we about to need some?"

"How can I hurry if . . . ? No! What about a baby sitter—the mother and father are off on an antique car trip somewhere between Lewiston and Whitebird—left three kids with a sitter. Boy got hurt and needs surgery—"

"Who says?"

"I say, first. Shaw agrees. Greenstick fracture of both bones in right leg above the ankle. Fell off a trampoline or something. Anyway, who signs for surgery? Shaw says it's an emergency."

"It is, in a way. Also an invitation to a lawsuit."

"He thinks if he could locate the parents . . ."

"Telephone permission? No way. And don't dig up a grandmother, either. Not unless she can prove legal guardianship. Contact the highway patrol, bring one of the antiquers home to sign. Meanwhile keep the leg immobile and packed . . ."

She laughed, her clear, lovely laughter.

"And, Greta!" he called after her. "Draw up a letter for them to leave with the next baby sitter, giving her permission to sign for any surgery necessary."

"I'll tell this one," she promised. "When I get her recovered from her hysterics."

And then there was another case which they could not discuss, handle, or certainly settle over a pre-dinner cocktail. Clancy came home rather late one evening to find Gretchen sitting in the dark, shivering, no dinner being kept warm for him in the kitchen.

"I thought you weren't at home," he said crossly. "What's wrong with you? Have the Lorellas abandoned us?" He dropped his briefcase, hung his topcoat away, loosened his tie, turned on the TV and came back to her.

"*Is* something wrong?" he asked in rising concern. "Tell me, Greta."

She sat where she was, twisting and rolling a wad of Kleenex in her hands. "This time . . ." she faltered. "This time I am really through with medicine."

"Oh, blazes! Who is it this time? Shaw? Fielder . . . ?"

"Cobbins," she said hoarsely. "Me. I'll be sued for malpractice, and I won't have any choice."

"How can you be sued for malpractice? You don't practice."

"Oh, I do, too. I watch postoperative patients and see that the charts are kept. And if a patient comes out of anesthesia fighting and thrashing around, I'm to blame if he stirs up a ventral hernia. And nobody can blame Keen or Shaw or anybody else who wasn't even in the hospital. But *I* was there. I was to blame."

He sat down on the big footstool before the couch. "Now tell me what happened. And why isn't there any dinner?"

She stood up. "I'll fix you something. That's the least I can do. I came home so upset—I told the Lorellas we wouldn't need them this evening—"

"Are they in their trailer?"

"I suppose so, the way it's raining. But don't get them, Clancy. I'll fix something for you."

"And you."

"I can't eat.

"All right, then. If it's that serious, tell me exactly what happened at the hospital today."

Her eyes dark and wide, for a long minute she gazed at him. "It began almost a week ago," she said, as if she herself did not believe what she said.

"And you've been sitting on it that long?" He sounded angry.

"Oh, no! Oh, *no*, Clancy! When it began—this man—

he drives a taxi, or a truck, or something. When he came in, his trouble was diagnosed as a case of acute appendicitis, and he was operated on. That was five days ago. The man asked for special nurses, but they were not available. They often are not, Clancy."

"But so far so good, eh?"

She glanced up at him. "Yes. I was on floor duty, surgical patients, so I came into it. After surgery, Dr. Shaw and Mrs. Keen looked at the patient—I saw them come out of his room. They left routine orders, and then went off somewhere."

"Out of the hospital?"

"Oh, yes. Everything did seem normal. The floor nurses were watching the man, taking temperature regularly, checking on the i.v. I myself had looked in on him twice."

She fell silent, and Clancy waited.

"I'm sorry," she said. "I should be feeding you."

"Tell me the rest. What happened?"

"Oh, yes. Well, almost immediately—he was just getting conscious. Almost immediately after Shaw and Keen had seen him, he was coming out of the anesthesia, and the nurse called me because the man was getting excited, thrashing about, and fighting us. When he became really violent, I sent for an orderly, and we eventually had to use restraints . . ."

"Tied him down?"

"Yes, and hobbled his limbs. We don't like to do that, but after surgery . . ."

"You don't have a recovery room?"

"We have one, but Shaw sends cases like this to their own rooms for duty care."

"I see. And that was five days ago?"

"Yes, but the family says now that I was at fault because he was allowed to become violent."

"You?"

"Well, the doctor in charge. And since Shaw and Keen had left—"

"What happened to him? Something must have happened."

"It did. Today Dr. Shaw discovered a ventral hernia. The family, when told that further surgery would be needed, said they would sue for malpractice. Sue the hospital and the doctor. Shaw says that is me."

"What do you think?"

"I told you what I thought. I did the best I could. If his thrashing about caused the hernia . . ."

"Did it?"

"I don't know. And if I was not competent, Shaw and Keen should have stuck around. But that's not what they think."

"I see."

"Clancy . . . ?"

He stood up. "How about fixing me some dinner? I have to think about this."

"Do you think I'm to blame?"

"I am sure you didn't intentionally refuse care to a patient."

"Oh, no, I didn't. And we got him restrained before too long."

"Dr. Shaw was told about his violence?"

"Of course. He asked if the man had quieted."

"This was by telephone."

"Yes."

"He had left— How soon after the surgery?"

"Oh, less than half an hour. But he and Keen always get away quickly."

"Dr. Shaw did not return to the hospital? After you called him?"

"Not until evening."

"All right. I think I have the picture. Now—food!"

She smiled weakly and went toward the kitchen. For a quick minute, she thought that she would get the Lorellas back—but she *couldn't* do that! It was her own fault that Clancy had no hot dinner waiting for him, that she herself had not eaten since a sandwich at eleven-thirty. So—

She looked into the refrigerator, into the freezer—on the shelves where were kept certain things in cans with which to feed unexpected visitors. She took down a can of black bean soup; she found lamb chops in the frig, and frozen peas—a pound cake, and a small dish that held frozen-but-now-thawed strawberries.

The chops went on the broiler; she put place mats on the kitchen counter.

She heard Clancy's voice and she went toward the family room, thinking that he was talking to her. He was not; he was on the phone. Going through the dining room, she opened the breakfront and took out two Chinese bowls, thin, translucent, decorated in soft green on white.

"This is Clancy Cobbins, here, sir," she heard her husband say. "Well, I'm fine, sir. Busy. An attorney keeps busy around here as long as there are water rights to litigate."

Gretchen took the bowls to the kitchen, looked at the

chops, and came back for napkins.

"I have a question I want to ask you, sir," Clancy was saying. "You said I might . . . Yes, sir."

"Well, you know that my wife is a doctor?"

"Yes, you were here for the wedding. I remember."

"Yes, she is stunning. And this question has come up. You see . . ."

Back in the kitchen, Gretchen opened the soup, put the peas on to cook, turned the chops, and came back.

"No," Clancy was saying. "She was not the surgeon. But she was on duty . . ."

Clancy was taking charge. Things would be all right. Gretchen filled the coffeepot and sliced the pound cake. She must tell Delmo that she had used the lamb chops.

Clancy came strolling out to the kitchen, a drink in his hand. He offered Gretchen a sip and she accepted. "Feeling better?" he asked.

"A little."

"I called my old boss in Denver."

"Did you really?"

"Yes. He knows all about most everything, especially malpractice suits, damages, and so on. And he says your taxi driver should sue the surgeon and the anesthetist, not you. You were working under their orders."

"But they can't be blamed, Clancy. They had left the hospital before the patient began to recover. They always do."

"That can be proven?"

"I suppose so. Their sign-out time, my chart record. But I let the man thrash around."

"And stopped it. Judge Decker says the family may have a case. But not against you unless he, and Shaw, could prove that the violence caused the hernia."

"What else?"

"Can they also prove there was not another cause?"

Gretchen stared at him.

"Judge Decker says there could be other causes. The man could have coughed."

"Yes, he could have. He yelled, too."

"That means strain. The Judge mentioned the condition of the skin where the incision was made."

"Oh, Clancy!"

"I tell you, he knows about these cases. He thinks your man has a case, but that he'd do better to sue the surgeon and the anesthetist for abandonment, and the hospital for its regulations, rather than you or the orderly because the half-conscious man did some thrashing about."

"But he was allowed . . ."

"Are you ready for me to eat?"

She served the soup, and perched on the stool beside Clancy. Gently he helped her take off the white jacket which she had worn home from the hospital. Under it she was wearing a blouse patterned in light red, and a dark red skirt.

"I panicked," she said apologetically. She knew that he thought she should leave her uniform at the hospital. "When Shaw told me . . . He said I was hysterical."

"Were you?"

"Maybe. I ran home."

"He knows he's in trouble."

"And Keen."

"Yes. But Shaw is the doctor of record."

"Yes, but if they sue the hospital and I was on duty . . ."

"Eat your soup."

She did eat some of it, stealing glances at her husband beside her.

"Look, Greta," he said when she was serving the lamb chops and the peas, the hot rolls, "think back five days. Did you do any harm to that man?"

"No-o. I did all I knew how to do. But the point is, Clancy, I do not know enough! I have not had enough training. I've not been working enough to get the experience I need. Did you know that Kathy Bennett was brought into the hospital yesterday as an acute alcoholic? My best friend! I should have been able to help her. But I didn't know enough there, either."

He let her talk. She was arguing now, and eating, too. The hysteria was about gone.

When she moved again, to bring the dessert and coffee, he said mildly, "You say you need more experience . . . Couldn't you get that?"

"Not now. It's too late."

"Oh, Gretchen. I think you can learn what you need to know."

"You mean, go back to school? Intern someplace, if any place would have me?"

He laughed. "You are sorry for yourself, aren't you?"

"That's what I need. Or I could surrender my license and stop calling myself an M.D."

"Do you want to do that?"

"No. No, I don't. Not really."

"All right. Eat your strawberries. We can take our coffee in to the fire. I'll go light it."

She made quick work of putting the dishes into the washer, and joined him. He drew her down beside him and said, "I think there is a way out of your dilemma, Gretchen."

"The lawsuit?"

"No. The insurance lawyers will handle that. I'll put a bug in their ears. I was talking about your abysmal ignorance."

She laughed a little.

"I have something to tell you," he said. "You would have learned it in staff meeting soon, anyway."

"If I go back."

"Oh, you're going back. Because my news is that a new doctor is coming in, to be Chief of Staff at the hospital."

She was astonished. That word had long been awaited —with dread, hope, every emotion. "I can't believe it!" she exclaimed. "Clancy, you wouldn't— Tell me, is he a good doctor? I mean—"

"I know what you mean. Yes, he is a 'good' doctor. An M.D."

"But— Why would he be coming here? We aren't very big; we are pretty isolated. We— Has he seen the hospital?"

"Yes. Til Holt took him around."

"Til?"

"You weren't on duty. This man is a friend of Til's parents. He came here, met with the Board, saw the hospital. He knows the building and equipment are good."

"Did he meet any of the staff?" Her tone was dark.

"Just as a visitor. A guest of Til's who was showing him the city's assets."

"Well, we do have a handsome building."

"Yes. And in a very nice town, Gretchen."

"Oh, I know that. But to come in as Chief of Staff when that staff has so many holes in it."

"Such a situation might present a challenge to the right man. And this doctor— I told you he was a friend of Til's parents?"

"Is he old?"

"No. Til is only thirty."

"I know . . ."

"This fellow— His name is Webbe, by the way. And it seems that he has some personal problems of his own—"

"That's all we need. A Chief with problems."

"Don't prejudge. I was favorably impressed with him. What he said about wanting a quieter place to work. He's been chief of his service in a very large teaching hospital . . ."

"What's his specialty?"

"He's a pediatrician."

"Oh, *Clancy!*"

"A surgeon, with all those Fellow and Diplomate things doctors string after their names."

She said nothing.

"Don't worry about it, Greta. I think he'll make a fine chief. The Board approved without dissent. And they asked him if he could bring in other qualified M.D.'s. They mentioned our present imbalance."

"Mhmmmn. Didn't he ask to meet the staff?"

"He did meet some of them. Just as a visitor, but he talked to them. And my thought is, Greta: Shouldn't you stand ready, offer to work with this man as you worked with Wagner, and that way learn the things you say you need?" His eyes alertly studied her face.

"Well . . ." she said slowly. "It seems good, but there would be a hundred things to consider. I'd need to meet him first, and he needs to meet me."

"But you would keep that course in mind?"

"I always try to do the things you want me to do." It was as far as she would commit herself. They listened to the night news, and then decided to go to bed. Clancy asked about Kathy, and Gretchen told him what little she knew. She had collapsed at some party, and been brought in.

Once in bed—Clancy always had a stack of books on his bed table, Gretchen had one which, that night, she did not touch. She lay for a few minutes looking up at the rain which made bright rivulets down the dark glass of the skylight.

"This doctor . . ." she said slowly. "Webbe. Is he any good? Really?"

Clancy used his forefinger to mark the place in his book. "I helped pick him," he said. "Do you remember that two-day trip I took earlier this month?"

"Yes, you said it was business."

"And you thought it was Susan's business."

"I didn't mention her name."

"You didn't need to. And you fed me liver the night I came home."

Gretchen giggled. "It's good for you."

"Well, a couple of the Board members interviewed possibilities for the job. There had been a lot of preliminary telephoning, writing, checking on credentials, and so forth. These were personal interviews."

"Who went with you?"

"Jonah IntVeld and Laura Motteline."

"Hmmmmn."

"She's on the Board, Gretchen, and works at it."

"I know."

"We had the prospectives come to Kansas City. We thought it would be a mistake to gather them here."

"Small-town talk."

"We have to deal with several angles, you know. Small city is one of them. Three of the staff men had wanted the position, had asked for it."

"I know that. Go on."

"Well, I interviewed Webbe first, and then brought the other Board members in. I definitely felt that he had the smarts to do the job."

She laughed at his slang.

"The point is, Jonah and Laura agreed with me. It was Laura who was impressed with the work he's done on preemies. That's premature . . ."

"I know what preemies are, Clancy!"

He grinned at her. "I'll bet you do. Well, he had done some fine surgery on them. I tell you, the man is good!"

"But didn't he want to look over the staff?"

"We didn't mince words telling him what we had."

"Including me?" She was half-ashamed of her feeling; it was more fright than anything else. But he might have discussed the thing with her! After all, she had been working as a doctor, she, too, was on the staff!

"I'm telling you now," he reminded her, guessing at her resentment.

"Well," she tried to explain, "if I am to work with the man—and the others, too, of course—we would have liked to be asked our opinion."

He smiled at her. "Some hospitals, I understand, are

run by Boards that include staff men. As a matter of fact, Wagner was on the Board. And Webbe will be."

"Okay," she said. "Read your book. I'll shut up."

"I think you'll like our new man, Greta." He spoke softly.

"What if I don't take up your educational project with him?"

He opened the book and settled into the pillows. "I'll see that you do."

"Threats."

"I won't need them. You'll like Webbe. I'll bet on that."

"In all your investigation, didn't you find out how old the man is? Exactly."

"Yes. He's fifty."

"Hmmmn. That's not so very old for a man who has made a name for himself. Can I read up on him?"

"I'd think so."

"Is he good-looking?"

"Well—in an ascetic sort of way."

She made a derisive sound.

"I'm not good at descriptions. He's tall, thin, with dark hair—and—and those sunken sort of cheeks."

"A skeleton could beat that," she laughed.

"His cheeks were red. His features well-cut. He wears dark-rimmed glasses—rather large lenses."

She reached for her own book. "I was going to ask—what if the man should fall in love with me? Teaching me, and all that there. But it doesn't sound as if I'd need to be concerned."

"I only hope you're good enough for him to bother with you at all," Clancy said stiffly.

She laughed aloud. "Me?" she asked. "Or my doctoring?"

"Oh, Gretchen, shut up!"

"Yes, sir. I shall do that, sir!"

"Anyway," said Clancy, still grumpily, "the man's married."

"So?" asked Gretchen, her voice cool.

Clancy laughed and shook his head. "Let's go to sleep," he said. "Don't forget to take your jacket when you go to the hospital tomorrow."

"I won't. I put it in my car."

CHAPTER 8

A WEEK passed before the announcement was made to the staff that a new doctor-in-charge had been secured and would arrive shortly. A brief résumé was made of this man. His name, Dr. McKinney Webbe. Where he had been educated, where he had been serving as chief of pediatric surgery. He was a Fellow in surgery, a Diplomate in pediatrics. He was married, with three grown children.

Gretchen listened to the comments of the staff men and of the rest of the hospital personnel. She said nothing about Clancy's having told her previously about Dr. Webbe. She wondered if he would be good enough to counteract all the prejudging that was going on.

"This puts me in my place!" said Dr. Shaw angrily. "A baby doctor!" But Shaw was also smarting over the insurance settlement to the taxi driver, and the Board's censure of him and Mrs. Keen for leaving the hospital too soon after that surgery. There was as well the recommendation that the Recovery Room be used for all postoperative patients. "If we need a new man so bad, why doesn't he get here and save some lives?"

Gretchen's friend Kathy decided that she didn't want to stay in the hospital, and her husband did not insist that she do so. But she did stay in the city, at her mother's house, and Gretchen remembered her decision to try to do something for the young woman. "If Til would have married her . . ." she said regretfully to Clancy.

"Look, old girl. I think Kathy herself knows that probably the strongest reason for Til not to consider marrying her was that she was a lush."

"She was crazy about him; maybe she still is. She would have stopped drinking . . ."

"Maybe."

Yes. Maybe. But on that Sunday evening—

A group of congenial men had gone to Denver to attend an "important" football game, Clancy and Hugh Purser among them. Mary Purser agreed to stay with Gretchen while they were gone. The men would return late on Sunday night.

Mary enjoyed her own small vacation in her daughter's home. The Lorellas made her comfortable; it was wonderful to visit with Gretchen, to be her guest. And on Sunday afternoon when Kathy drove her big car up before the house, she was ready to assent to Gretchen's suggestion that they be nice to Kathy.

"At least she won't be drinking," she said naively. "It does worry her mother . . ."

"I should think so," said Gretchen, going to open the front door. The Lorellas had the afternoon and evening free.

Kathy blew in on a blast of cold air. The temperature had been dropping for two days; there was heavy snow in the higher elevations and a few flakes blew about there in the valley. Kathy had pinned her black hair back from her face, her dark skin was an unhealthy color; there were dark circles under her enormous eyes.

"Oh, hello, Gretchen's mother!" she greeted Mrs. Purser—a greeting which carried over from her very small childhood. She stood uneasily, glancing at Gretchen, then away. "I thought," she said, "we could go somewhere for dinner."

"It's snowing," said Mrs. Purser.

"Not much. We could drive to that new motel and shopping center over at Durell."

"That's forty miles, isn't it, Kathy?"

Kathy turned her back on her. But she was sober, and Gretchen wanted her to stay that way. "Where's Barney?" she asked.

"Playing poker. He does most weekends. Unless at harvest time. Can't we go, Gretch?"

Gretchen didn't want to. Mary Purser definitely did not. But—"We could go somewhere," she agreed. "Though if you don't want to, Mother . . ."

Mrs. Purser got up to fetch her coat. "It's going to storm," she said. "That snow's been working itself down here since yesterday noon."

"Yes, I know," said Gretchen, following her. "We won't take any chances. But Kathy does need to be kept busy."

"She looks terrible, Gretchen."

"She always looks terrible. She's a rancher now."

Kathy's hair was wisping about her face; she wore a plaid wool jacket and jeans. Boots. Gretchen had a fur jacket over tailored slacks. Mary wore a cashmere coat and scarf. They all sat in the front seat of the car, and Gretchen closely watched Kathy's driving.

Out on the highway she mentioned the blowing snow. "I don't think we'll make it to the shopping center," she told Kathy.

Kathy drove for another ten miles. The snow fell more thickly.

"Kathy," said Gretchen. "We should turn back."

"Oh, Gretch . . ."

"I say we should, too," said Mrs. Purser. "That's two against one, Kathy."

Without a word of protest or agreement, Kathy jerked the wheel and swung the car in a wide curve; she cut across the median strip and started back to the city. Mary Purser leaned back, her eyes closed. Gretchen pointed to the speedometer. "Now you slow down, Kathy Bennett!" she said sternly. "If there had been any other fools out on the road, you would have killed us all."

"Who'd care?"

"I'd care. Dad and Clancy would care. Now, take us home, or to the hotel. We can eat there."

"The hotel dining room isn't open on Sunday evenings."

"There's that seafood place."

"I don't like fish."

"All right. How about the Steak House?"

To her relief, Kathy agreed. "I'll drive after this," Gretchen whispered to her mother.

"She's crazy."

"Sick."

The Steak House was popular, run by a retired army colonel and his wife, with good food available. Mary

Purser said she wanted a bowl of soup, Gretchen ordered a steak sandwich, and Kathy did the same, though she would want dessert.

"Where is everybody?" she asked, looking around the half-filled dining room.

"They all know it is going to storm. Eat your sandwich, Kathy."

"I want some wine."

"Try coffee."

"Oh, Gretchen. Always preaching."

"I don't like drunks."

"We used to be friends."

"Dry up, and we can be again."

"Doesn't she talk to me awful, Mrs. Purser?"

Mary just smiled; she was not enjoying their expedition. "They make good soup here," she said to Gretchen.

"I know they do. What are you going to have for dessert, Kathy?"

The waitress brought the list, which was long. "Champagne sherbet!" announced Kathy, giggling. "Only it doesn't have any champagne in it."

"It's good though. Mother and I will have it. Do you . . . ?"

Kathy was on her feet. "I have to go get some gas," she said, starting down the room. "My tank reads empty."

"She'll find a drink somewhere," said Gretchen. "And we're left with the check."

"How will we get home?"

"Call a cab."

They ate their sherbet, pink and refreshing, and Gretchen asked the waitress for the check. The proprietor himself brought it. "Mrs. Binnard told me to make separate checks," he said.

Gretchen laughed. "That's one way to take your friends to dinner," she said. "I'll pay the whole thing. And we'll need a cab. I don't think Mrs. Binnard will be back."

"She's parking her car at the door right now," said Colonel Schuler. "It's snowing harder."

"I'll still pay the whole check."

Evidently he told Kathy that, because she came to the table announcing that she'd had to get nineteen and a half gallons of gas. "And at these prices . . . Thanks, Gretch. I'll pay you for my share."

Gretchen looked at her. "How much does your gas tank hold?" she asked.

"Twenty gallons."

"And you were starting down the Interstate to drive forty miles? Kathy, you're crazy!"

"You bet," said Kathy, laughing loudly, tossing her loosened black hair back from her face.

"If her husband is any kind of a man . . ." Mary Purser said to her daughter.

"He isn't, Mother. Now, I'm going to hurry out to the car. I plan to drive us home."

Kathy gave no argument. She had had her drink, and willingly crawled into the back seat.

"I'll speak to her mother," said Mary Purser when they were safely back in the Cobbinses' house. Kathy had driven away.

"You won't do any such thing," said Gretchen, "because, for one thing, Mrs. Bennett knows anything you can tell her. Now! Shall I take you home? Or will you stay for this night, too? And Stephen will take you in the morning. I go on duty at seven."

She did go on duty at seven, with four inches of snow on the ground, her wooded mountainside a fairy place. She was working steadily at the hospital, serving one day out of ten with the mobile unit, not letting herself be upset by the rising need she saw in the hospital for Dr. Webbe to arrive.

"He's creating suspense," she told Clancy.

"Maybe. I just think he is finding it hard to get things in order to leave."

"What things?"

"His hospital affairs, and family matters as well, probably his house to sell . . ."

"I see."

But the day came when Dr. Webbe did arrive. Quietly, without fanfare. This slender, tall man just showed up at the seven-thirty staff briefing.

He looked at the four men and the handsome young woman seated at one end of the table. The doctors. At the supervisor of nurses and the business administrator of the hospital.

He nodded. "I am Mac Webbe," he said quietly. "I have come to be Chief of Staff of the hospital here. I think you know where I have been working, what I've been doing. Well, I think the past twenty years of my life have been misspent. I have worked in a huge hospital complex, with every specialist, lab test and gadget at my disposal. Now I want to work close to the patients, and find out if I am a doctor on my own. I'll use instruments, we'll use lab tests, but this is going to be one hospital where only the really sick and injured are cared for, where the doctors' main efforts will be to care for the people in these beautiful mountains in their homes, taught by us to make themselves well, and how to stay well.

"I've already started along this line by giving the babies back to their mothers as soon as they are born, to nurse and to care for. We make deliveries in the hospital for the doctors' convenience, and I may stop even that out here.

"Now let me see if I have your names straight . . ."

He did have. He gave each one his attention, Gretchen no more than Dr. Fielder. He then turned the staff meeting back to the staff, sat turned halfaway from the table, watching and listening.

Gretchen studied him. Clancy had given her an unskilled but accurate picture of the man. He was very clean. His lab coat was tailored, under it his shirt collar showed starchy smooth, his blue and white striped tie was precisely knotted. His hair was thick, with a controlled wave, dark blond in color. Behind his eyeglasses, his eyes were keen. He had little to say until Gretchen said she had met up with a situation the day before. She turned to Dr. Webbe. "I was on duty with the mobile unit," she explained.

"I'll want to hear more about that unit," he said. "But give us your situation first."

"Yes, sir. I had three patients come in, each telling me that he had had treatment from a Dr. Warrington. One had had prescriptions for pneumonia, another had an injured leg dressed."

"Adequately?"

Gretchen shrugged. "The point is, sir, I don't think this Warrington is a doctor. You see . . ." She went on to detail the experiences Susan had had with the man. "My husband is Mrs. Warrington's attorney, and he thought he had the man stopped in these parts. He thought—at least he hoped that the Veterans Hospital was caring for his mental problem. He must have been discharged."

"Have you told your husband?"

"I shall. I was warning the hospital here, and I'll report the matter to the unit's sponsors. A pretend-doctor is not what we need in any of our health projects."

"Did you think any damage was done to the patients you saw?"

"Not that I could see. He's a smart man, I believe. But if he's treating patients and writing prescriptions . . ."

"Yes, of course. Thank you for warning us. Now, can someone tell me briefly about this mobile unit? I have had it mentioned, and it sounds as if it were already starting the kind of work I want to do out here. Dr. Shaw . . . ?"

Dr. Shaw laughed shortly. "Don't look at me. Ask Gretchen; she gets credit for starting that project."

Dr. Webbe looked again at the young woman who sat at the far corner of the table. She was beautiful, and had spoken well about the impostor doctor. Shaw evidently did not like her. The new chief waited.

Gretchen spoke slowly, thoughtfully, turning to look at the new man, thus presenting her shoulder to Shaw. "I got some credit," she admitted, "because I had happened, that year, to be elected President of the Four

County Medical Society, and the society sponsored—it still sponsors—the unit." Speaking more swiftly, she told what the trailer was and had, detailed its itinerary and its services.

"Is it affiliated with our hospital here?" asked Dr. Webbe.

"Not formally, sir. We use this hospital in referring patients, and for consultation."

"And you give your time?"

"I do that on my free days."

"But our doctors . . . ?"

"Dr. Fielder does the same thing, yes." She smiled at the old man. "At first Dr. Giamonco did some work. Dr. Wagner worked with the unit, and Dr. Tipton did until he left."

"I see."

There was a heavy silence. Dr. Webbe gathered his notes and thanked the staff. Everyone scattered.

"Dr. Cobbins," said the chief as Gretchen was leaving.

She turned.

"I gather," said Dr. Webbe, "that the D.O.'s on our staff do not belong to this mobile unit project. Shouldn't they?"

"They don't belong to the Four County Medical Society either," said Gretchen.

"Don't they have the same licensure in this state as the M.D.'s?"

"Yes, sir. But they have their own organization, and I suppose they could start their own mobile unit."

"You mentioned Giamonco. Don't the others offer to help with the unit?"

"They haven't as yet," said Gretchen.

"Do you get along with them? You and Dr. Fielder?"

"Fielder gets along with anybody. I have some problems, but possibly not because of my M.D."

Dr. Webbe smiled. "We'll talk about this again."

"Yes, sir. Meanwhile . . ."

"Continue as you have been doing, Doctor. I want everyone to do that, so that I can evaluate the job I have in hand."

"Yes, sir." It was, she decided, not the time to talk to him about "interning" under him.

And a little time was to pass before she did meet up with that good opportunity. She told Clancy about Warrington, and found that Dr. Webbe had already reported the matter.

And two days later, Kathy Binnard came to the hospital, not to see Gretchen, but to see Dr. Leavitt, Ob.-Gyn. Only by chance, Gretchen met her in the hall.

"What are you doing here?" she asked, surprised.

"Barney made me come. Last Sunday you were so cross with me."

"Last Sunday" had been three weeks ago! The snow had melted, and more had come.

"I would have told you then, but I decided you wouldn't help me."

"Oh, Kathy!"

"You just fuss because I drink a little."

"I fuss because you drink a lot!"

"Well, anyway—I didn't tell you that I was pregnant, and—"

Gretchen turned white. "That you are . . . ?"

Kathy tried to face her defiantly. "It happens," she said.

"Yes, I know, but— Oh, *Kathy!*"

"You know what?" Kathy giggled. "That Leavitt guy, he thought I wanted an abortion."

"And you didn't."

Kathy gazed at her solemnly. "He said it would be a good idea. But— Oh, Gretchen, I don't know what I want. Except I wish you could be my doctor. Could you?"

Now Gretchen was into it! She must find an answer for Kathy. This matter was not one to take to Clancy, as she had been taking her other little messes. This one—

"I'd rather have you, Gretchen," Kathy persisted.

"All right, all right! Let me think."

If she asked Kathy to wait while she talked to Dr. Webbe— It would take time to explain to him now the things she should have set out for him at once. She must tell him about Kathy, and—oh, the whole thing.

She kept Kathy close, and went to the house telephone.

Yes, Dr. Webbe would see her and the patient. She took Kathy to a restroom and bathed her face, combed her hair. "Don't try to talk," she said. "You only get excited . . ."

In the fifteen minutes they had to wait on the Chief, Gretchen made up her mind on what she would say to the new man. When his secretary said they could go in, she was ready. "I'll talk to Dr. Webbe alone first," she said. "See that Mrs. Binnard doesn't leave." She turned to Kathy. "You will wait, won't you, Kathy?"

Kathy had picked up a magazine, and she shrugged. "If you're not too long."

"I won't be." She pushed through to Dr. Webbe's office, flushed with all the things she wanted to get said and done in a short time.

She knew that she was lecturing. But there was the time element, and so many things to say. She must explain her medical status to the quiet, watchful man behind the desk. "Eyeglasses so big and bright do conceal a person's thoughts," she managed to note.

She said that she had been learning practical hospital service under Dr. Wagner. "It was a deep personal shock when he died," she explained. "I have hoped that you would continue what he began. The other men on the staff . . ." She said only a little about those men. "I have never worked with D.O.'s before. Perhaps I am to blame that we don't get along better." It did not occur to her to mention the taxi driver's appendix. But she did tell about Kathy, her "best friend" since babyhood. "We lived on the same street, did everything together. Until I went away to college, and medical school, then married. Now she is married to a rancher. In the last years, she has changed. She drinks too much. And now she says she is pregnant. She came to Dr. Leavitt here. He seems to think she wants an abortion."

"Does she?"

"I asked her and she said she didn't know what she wanted."

Dr. Webbe stirred then. He sat up straight in his desk chair and drew a large pad of paper forward. "Perhaps an abortion is what your friend does need, Doctor," he said.

"She's outside."

"I'll see her later, if that seems necessary. I want first

to determine what your problem is."

Gretchen stared at him.

"If this woman is your friend, and you knew that she was an alcoholic, why didn't you try to do something to help her before she became pregnant?" His tone was quiet, spoken almost in a monotone.

Gretchen was shocked. "She was my friend, not my *patient*, Dr. Webbe!"

"I take the position, Doctor, that everyone is every doctor's patient."

"But . . ."

He noted her shock, and he smiled a little. "You asked me for instruction, Dr. Cobbins. You may not want me to say this, but I feel that Dr. Leavitt was correct in suggesting an abortion for your friend. I have done enough work with fetal alcoholics that I would observe Mrs. Binnard's pregnancy as too risky to continue. The syndrome's pattern is distressingly clear. And we are sure it begins in the womb. The risk of bearing physically and mentally deficient offspring, or children who die very soon, is too great a one to take. I think you should talk to the husband and to her parents, maybe before you talk to the patient. Tell them the risks which a chronically alcoholic mother runs."

Gretchen had a swift, swirling picture of telling the Bennetts these awful things. Even Vera's broad, smiling face came into the kaleidoscope.

"I can't do that!" she cried. "I couldn't go to Kathy's parents . . . And I hardly know her husband!"

Dr. Webbe stood up. "A doctor does not need to *know* a patient's husband, Dr. Cobbins, to make a report on a case. As for her parents— What sort of friend are you to these people? What sort of *doctor* are you? What sort of doctor do you want me to train you to be?"

Gretchen felt as if she had been through an earthquake or a tornado. "I never had anyone talk to me that way before!" she told Clancy when, finally, she told him about Kathy.

"What is Kathy going to do?" he asked.

"Binnard says she should have the abortion."

"What are you advising? Didn't she come to you for advice?"

"Yes, she did. But, Clancy . . ."

"Calm down now. Put on your boots and your coat. We'll take a walk."

They took their walk, up the road and across the field to "their mountain." When they came back, with red cheeks, their arms were full of small branches of spruce, broken off in the heavy snow of last week.

"I wish," said Clancy, putting these neatly into the kindling well of their fireplace, "that you would invite Webbe to dinner some night next week."

Gretchen gasped, and dropped her branches on the floor. "You *what?*" she cried.

Clancy glanced around at her. "I'd like you to do that," he said.

Gretchen took off her jacket and busied herself cleaning up the mess she had made. After the things that man had made her say to poor Kathy . . . "Do you know," she asked, outraged, "that he never calls me anything but *Doctor* Cobbins?"

Clancy laughed. "You're rotten spoiled!" he told her.

CHAPTER 9

GRETCHEN made no plans to invite Dr. Webbe to dinner, but she watched the man, listened to him, and hung back from close contact with him. He had not committed himself about the teaching she had asked him to do, but she was learning many things from him.

He was being widely entertained, and when invited, Clancy insisted that she accept and go with him to the parties. "People like Webbe," he said. "I like him."

Gretchen said nothing.

Dr. Webbe was working hard at the hospital; there seemed to be nothing he was not ready to do. Changes were made, suggestions considered and accepted. He attended a meeting of the medical society. He said he probably soon would have things in shape so that he could help with the mobile unit. He said he thought they should encourage any D.O. who wanted to join. "At least ask them," he said. "We don't have so many of them in this district."

At a hospital staff meeting—he held these regularly—tissue meetings, journal meetings, full staff rap and bitch meetings—meetings when he would address the group on some hospital change or on a medical service—he announced that he hoped he had "snagged" an internist. "A fella who's done a good bit of study and work with the heart. He has an asthmatic child, and he feels our thin mountain air will benefit the kid."

"Now it's *his* air," said Dr. Giamonco in Gretchen's ear as the meeting broke up.

"Oh, shut up!" said Gretchen crossly. "There's enough to go 'round."

Dr. Webbe had been with them for a month when Gretchen felt that she had her first real involvement with the man. Later, thinking about it, she decided that he had led her into the experience, to teach her, to talk to her.

A case had come into the hospital, a man who had been a patient there before because of a heart condition, arrhythmia. Now he had been brought in again, and after twenty-four hours, he died.

Gretchen was the one to pronounce death, and to fill out the forms. She was aware of Dr. Webbe's presence behind her as she wrote.

"Did you know this man?" the Chief asked unexpectedly.

Gretchen looked up at him. "I knew him," she said. "Not well. He was priest at St. Joseph's for several years. We . . ."

"I know you are not Catholic."

Gretchen turned back to her records.

"Had he been a patient here before? Did you know him then?"

"Yes. But there, again, not well. He was Dr. Tipton's

patient." Webbe probably had seen the man's records, but it was not her place to remind him of that.

"I am going to do an autopsy," said the Chief of Staff. "When you finish there, come down and help me."

Oh, boy!

While in medical school, Gretchen had watched one autopsy. She did not want to see another, let alone *help* . . . She could just see Clancy brush back his smooth brown hair, and hear him say, "You want to be taught."

Well, she did. And in that autopsy room, probably alone with Dr. Webbe . . .

Grudgingly from the first, though the pace was picking up, she was coming to know this man. Well, not *know* . . . but certainly to admire him, his ways, and his work.

She dreaded the autopsy, but soon lost any feeling except interest and admiration. An orderly assisted, and seemed as pleased as was Gretchen. "This guy knows his stuff!" he told her.

Dr. Webbe did know his "stuff." He worked deftly, neatly. He was a superb surgeon. Clearly, simply, he told Gretchen what he was doing, and why. He was, he said, particularly interested in the heart, in the blood vessels. "Tell me about him," he said again. "I know you didn't know him well. But what was his condition as a patient when he was here before? He had an irregular heartbeat. All right. Was his mood depressed? Exhilarated? What? This time, when he came in, you received him. What about his mood?"

The autopsy room was cold, lighted by wide-shaded drop bulbs. Water ran into the sinks, an instrument crashed against a pan's edge, feet scraped on the concrete floor. The doctors and the orderly were masked, gowned, gloved, and busy.

Dr. Webbe explained—commented, rather—on what he was doing.

"Can you dissect, Doctor?" he asked Gretchen. "But of course you can. Please get this artery, put it into solution in that pan. Now, this one—"

They worked, speaking quietly; finally Dr. Webbe said, as if satisfied, "I thought so!"

Gretchen looked across at him.

"About those moods," he said. "Tell me what you know. Before his earlier attack, before this one. You took the histories, didn't you?"

"Yes," said Gretchen. "Yes, sir, I did. I wrote down . . ."

"What sort of man was he, generally? As he lived, as he worked?"

Gretchen glanced at the towel-shrouded head of the man on the gray slab. "He was a priest," she said, "of St. Joseph's Church. He—I've heard people say he was a gloomy man, subject to spells of crankiness. The first attack—he said, himself, that he had been losing sleep over the rumor that his church was going to be closed."

"Go on," said Dr. Webbe.

"Well, he developed this irregular heartbeat, which must be frightening."

"It is. Was he angry over the church's closing?"

"Excited. He wanted to talk about it. And sit up . . ."

"Yes. And this time . . ."

"He wasn't angry but, again, he was excited. He'd just been told that he would be raised to monsignor, and he wanted to talk about that."

"Yes. A depressed man, angry, euphoric— We want to make a very careful report on this case, Doctor. You see, back in the large center where I have been working, a heart man is doing research on just such cases as we have here. If I can send him this case, he will add it to the twenty-six he already has of patients—men—in their fifties, high risk patients with a history of heart disease, who have been depressed for some time, experiencing a change of mood, anxiety, or anger—and then who die within twenty-four hours after the first significant symptoms of an attack. The theory is that the heart attacks are triggered by a sudden drop in pulse rate and blood pressure when the man relapses into his usual depressed—or gloomy—state after a short period of being aroused. The contrast is too much for the body already weakened by heart disease."

"Should we have done something when he was brought in?" asked Gretchen.

"Not more than was done. The availability of a telephone heart attack service or a mobile coronary care ambulance would not have made any difference for this man. Between his attacks, he was anxious, he was angry —but he was reluctant to ask a doctor to help. Right?"

"Yes. He had had no medical care, and was impatient when brought in yesterday. He said he did not have time to be sick."

"Yes!" said Dr. Webbe with satisfaction. He stripped off his gloves. "Well, we did a job here, didn't we? You wouldn't want to specialize in pathology, would you, Doctor?" he asked Gretchen.

She laughed. "Not if I have a choice. You'd do better to get someone who is already trained."

"I suppose." He made a last examination of the cadaver, touched the large, closing sutures, and he nodded to the orderly. "He can be moved. Thank you for your help."

"Yes, sir," said the man respectfully.

Gretchen took off her cap and her gown. "Dr. Webbe," she said, catching up with him before he reached the elevator. "My husband and I would like to have you come to our house for dinner one night next week. Could you?"

"I think so. Can you cook and make out reports, too?"

Gretchen smiled at him. "With help," she said gayly. "With help."

"Well, get that report sketched out for me first. And tell me when you've decided on the night."

He went one way, she another. Gretchen watched him go. Good gracious! she thought. What a reaction from the autopsy room! But that doctor, that *man!* She had not been in such a glow, she had not been swept along in such a force, since— Well, maybe she never had been! The man was fascinating! He *did* things! He had let her ask him to instruct and help, without comment. Then he had proffered her that instruction and help, still without comment . . .

Now! She must plan her dinner, she must make out the report, and both had better be good!

They were good. Dr. Webbe thanked her for the report, read it, and made no suggestions for additions or changes. "I'll put a note in and send it along," he said quietly. "Thank you, Doctor."

"Thank *you,* Doctor. Will you come for dinner Friday night?"

"Gretchen's parties are fabulous," Til Holt told Dr. Webbe as he took him to the house that evening. "Even the weather cooperates."

It was a crisp-cold night, with crunching snow on the ground, a thin, crescent moon high in the sky, and a dozen friends within the warm, fragrant house. Gretchen had borrowed her mother's cook to help Delmo. Delmo herself fascinated Dr. Webbe, as well as Gretchen's ability to communicate with the deaf woman.

The dinner table glowed with yellow damask and yellow Venetian glass. The flowers were blue lupine and pink-bronze roses, arranged around squat candlesticks that held tall yellow tapers.

The food—a clear, hot soup with floating slices of lemon and hard-boiled egg. Sautéed trout with lemon sauce, tiny new potatoes boiled in their jackets. Guinea hen and a hot compote of red cherries, green asparagus in Hollandaise. The dessert was vanilla ice cream with fresh strawberry sauce and macaroons. The coffee was perfect.

"Do I get to walk around the block after that dinner?" Dr. Webbe asked his hostess.

"It's required," she assured him.

The beautiful home, the company—it made a warm, gay scene which McKinney Webbe confessed surprised him. "Whatever happened to the Indians?" he asked.

"They are around," Clancy told him. "That dark-haired girl flirting with my father-in-law is one-half Shoshone."

Webbe was a social success, and he acknowledged that he enjoyed it. "Though I came out here to work," he said.

"And you do," murmured his hostess. He recognized and enjoyed the way she had maneuvered him to talk about his ideas as a pediatrician, the hopes he had of putting his ideas to work in the hospital and the community.

"The wine," he told her, "your good brandy. When do I get my walk?"

"After my mother and dad leave. Clancy will let us go, because I am working, and he encourages that."

"You can't walk far in that dress and those Band-Aids you call shoes."

"No, I can't, can I?" she agreed.

But they did walk. Gretchen changed into a red jump suit and heavy shoes. Webbe tried to explain to the remaining group around the fire.

"We know, we know!" said Jim Adams. "We've walked up the hill with Gretch in our time. It's because you love the mountains and the freedom out here. And especially the people!"

"Were they putting me on?" Webbe asked Gretchen when they started.

"Certainly. We speak out, we hill folk."

Clancy had provided Dr. Webbe with a short, fur-lined leather jacket, heavy gloves, and what he called mukluks over his shoes.

"I don't suppose we should walk too far," he suggested to Gretchen after they had gone up the hill far enough to look down at the smoke spiraling from the wide chimney of the Cobbins house.

"As far as we want to," she assured him. "That gang won't break up a minute before two A.M."

"They are interesting people."

"Yes, they are. And worthwhile people, most of them.

You seem to fit in."

"I'm glad you can tell me that."

They walked. They paused for breath, and talked. About Gretchen's home, and the dinner she had arranged. He spoke again about the contrast between the reality of life here in the valley and his preconceived ideas.

"I didn't really expect log cabins," he confessed.

"We have them, some pretty elegant."

But what did it matter, their talk and its subjects? The clear cold air, their closeness—Webbe would grasp Gretchen's hand to help him negotiate a steep stretch.

The stillness of the snow, the trees, the mountains, held them as in a crystal ball, through which they looked with wonder down on the lights of the valley, up at the stars in the deep blue vault of the sky.

Gretchen found all this exciting; she glowed inwardly with happiness and excitement. This man— There was something about him, not blatant, not very much of it, but it was there, that small, erotic promise. And it was exciting.

She felt sixteen again, thrilled with the thought of what might lie ahead.

And when, at last, they turned homeward, she said something of the sort to Mac Webbe.

He laughed. "I suspect you are flirting with me, Gretchen," he said deeply.

"Oh, no!" she cried. "I never flirt!"

"Because you never need to," he agreed, his tone still quiet.

"I seem to need to find some approach to you," she told him.

In the starlight, his smile was patient.

"I do," she insisted. "I've never known a man like you."

"Now I am sure you are not serious. I have seen your husband, and your friends. On the basis of age alone, I cannot compete."

"Oh," she threw that off, "I have always liked older men."

Like Valier, her memory intruded, and she shook her head free of the fur-lined hood.

"And then," Dr. Webbe was saying reasonably, "there is our married state. You knew I was married?"

"Did it make you blind?" she asked over her shoulder as she ran down a slope.

He caught up with her. "I've met your husband, remember. I like him. He's clever; he's a solid person. Why did you marry him, if—"

Clancy, the grocer boy. The cabin by the river, and—

"I don't think love was the real reason," said Gretchen soberly. She turned to look up, ready to argue, persuade. "How about you?" she asked. "Is that your situation?"

He made no answer; he walked down to her, took her arm, and led her quickly down, and down again to the road, to the house where two backgammon games and a wire corn popper were in operation.

Their friends looked up at their arrival. "Have some corn, Doc," said Jim Adams. "Both Docs."

Gretchen was able to greet her friends and blend in with their moods smoothly and gracefully. Dr. Webbe was not. For the next hour he was quiet, and he drove home with Til without saying one word.

"Quite an evening?" Til asked when he let him out at the hospital.

Dr. Webbe nodded, his mouth twisting wryly. "I won't get much sleep," he predicted, "with all I have to think about."

And he found that he was right. None of his usual devices worked. He could not sleep. He finally gave up and sat in the armchair which his room provided. "I'll have to get me an apartment or a house," he said aloud. "So I can roam."

Reading was no help, so he turned off the lamp and sat gazing out of the window—and thinking. *Is that your situation?* she had asked him.

His situation . . . Had he married for love? How did one answer that? What sort of love? At what time of his life had there been love? Did that time matter, or the time as of now?

But the question really was a simple one. He had asked Gretchen if she had married for love, and in turn she had asked him . . . So, what was the answer to that?

No, he could not claim that he had so married, that he had so stayed married, that—

He could think back over his life in the flash of seconds. But Gretchen . . . That took longer.

The young woman-doctor, walking, self-possessed, down the hospital corridor. The woman on the snowy mountainside tonight, her face shadowed in her fur-lined parka hood. The gracious hostess in a white frock that beautifully displayed her back and shoulders, her arms and her bosom. The crystal and the silver, the flowers that made a proper-seeming background for her. The fine, and handsome, husband whom Webbe had come to know and to like. The alcoholic Kathy, Gretchen's best friend, from babyhood. She had not attended the party. So there must be other pictures.

Gretchen's parents—the tall, eye-patched banker who stressed his also being a rancher. Her Dresden-doll mother.

What sort of woman was this Gretchen? What sort of doctor would she learn to be? What was her life really like?

He could not answer the questions that night, he could not escape them during the following week. On Friday he told the administrator that he was going to be away for a couple of days.

"Hunting, Dr. Webbe?"

"I have a borrowed camper. I've never shot a gun in my life. There is a fishing rod—if it were warmer, I might fish."

"You might catch something now in a still pool."

"All right. I may try."

He had a detailed map, food and shelter. It did not matter, really, where he went, what he did. He would not talk about his personal "situation," but he had found, this past week, that running away was not the whole answer to a problem. He must sometime think about that "situation" which Gretchen had introduced, and face what would come next. Because things would happen, decisions must be made. Steps taken.

"And the first one," he told himself as he drove along the winding road, "will not be an affair with a doctor on my staff, even if she is a tall, cool beauty with an exciting laugh and eager, inviting eyes."

He found a place in the National Forest where he could pull the camper under the trees, fill his coffeepot in the narrow, swift stream which came tumbling down over the rocks, watch a ground squirrel scrabble in the mast for hidden treasure, and sit on the camper's doorstep in the sun.

And think.

To go back:

Under these tall trees to the lush, blowing ones of a college campus nearly three thousand miles away. To a youth of twenty, studying fiercely to complete his pre-med work in three years. And to a girl. A girl with eyes that were a true turquoise, though she also had freckles, pale eyelashes and brows. Her hair was a dusty light red. She was not pretty, she made no attempt to be pretty. But she had a will . . .

She was content to sit beside the eye-glassed pre-med and study for her own exams. And when they were tired . . .

Had they married for "love"? Sex, certainly, and there had been an attraction. But love, and tenderness, no. From the first, they had fought like tigers.

"Why in hell did you think you had to marry her?" his father shouted at him.

But he had defied his father, his whole family. They had all but cut off his chance for a medical education which, even then, he had wanted more than Elise, more than any woman.

He and Elise. They had studied together, they had made love, and they married. It seemed simple at the time. It seemed simple now. But love? No.

Even the appeal of sex had soon vanished. It had been specious from the first. He could have had the same thing with a dozen students. Almost at once, Elise had given up her studies. He knew now that if his family's objection to his marriage had continued, and they had cut off his funds, she would have left him.

But the family did not hold out. They agreed to finance his studies. And her will again carried the two of them through those hard years. She read him clearly at all times. She still did. When it seemed to be too difficult to study medicine and earn money at some job at the same time, she had known that he would ask his parents for more help. She had learned that he would pay any price—humility, diminished pride, submission—to get what he wanted more than anything else—his medical studies, and then his work as a doctor, a surgeon.

Before he had finished his pre-med studies, a child was born. Having decided on pediatrics, he wanted children of his own, and he had paid a price for that. Was it worth what he paid? It was. It had been.

Until the last year or two. Then, firmly established in his career, he had had time to look analytically at the rest of his life. So he had come here to Idaho. Where there was work—and a young woman who seemed frankly to face life, and was ready, of herself, to reach out for what she wanted from it.

He realized that a chill was replacing the sun on his doorstep. The shadows of the mountains were turning blue-purple. Rising to the east was a cliff that went up and up into the darkening sky. Green lichen veined its walls of polished black basalt. At the foot of it the river ran like silver.

He stood up and walked a way to stir his blood, watching the shadows grow and deepen, seeing the sunlight creep up the cliff face.

Before it was entirely gone, he went back to the

camper, lighted the lantern and the stove; he cooked bacon and made coffee, opened a can of soup. "I should have brought at least one yellow candle," he told himself wryly. A week ago he had eaten dinner at a flower-decked table, drunk wine from yellow crystal that sparkled like frost, eaten crushed strawberries and smooth, rich ice cream. The warm, bare shoulders of beautiful women had been about him, the deep voices and strong laughter of men . . .

He rummaged in his grub sack, brought up an apple, and stretched out on the bunk. Later he would tidy the kitchen, and get into his sleeping bag. For now—

He ate his apple and made a real effort to go back, and back to his marriage of thirty years ago, to see things as they had happened to two young people. Then he, at least, had naively expected everything. He bravely faced earning their way, giving blood, doing odd jobs at the university, and taking extra duty in the hospital when finally he reached med school. It seemed, even then, that all glamor and excitement had quickly departed their marriage. Elise was older and probably had expected much more than the one room where they lived. Their meals were prepared on a two-burner stove, baths were taken down the hall, clothes laboriously washed there, or expensively at the Helpee Selfee. And always there were the long hours he must study. She had complained of the light, and he had studied at the library or down in the furnace room. Ill-fed, ill-clothed, tired all of the time. She had complained bitterly, and, looking back, he thought she had had a right to complain.

His parents could have provided a decent apartment for them, they could have bought him shoes when he needed them, a warm coat when the old one fell apart. But he was taking tuition, expensive books and lab fees from them, and would ask for nothing more.

They probably thought that Elise would contribute something, at least for that first year. She had not. She was no help then, or later.

When he developed pneumonia in his second year of med, she had defied him and gone to his parents. He was in the infirmary and eating what they fed him there. She had no money for food. There was the child—and Mac, she said, would have to work or give up his studies. He could not do both. She had been right, but what she did was wrong, because it convinced her that if she demanded it, money would be forthcoming.

And she was right. She made demands on his parents, and they came through. When he began to earn money, he must drive himself to make enough to satisfy her demands on him. He must choose where he worked, with whom he worked, with that need in mind.

Then the day came when he recognized the danger that he was running, tarnishing his ideals, sacrificing his standards. And he made a direct turnabout. He would specialize in pediatric surgery. He would pass the Boards. Yes, he would earn money, but probably not enough. Later, yes, there would be more. He would do demonstrations, he would address seminars.

Meanwhile Elise could manage as best she could on her own. He could provide her with a home, a fixed amount of money to spend on the things she seemed to enjoy. By then he knew too well that she was lazy, that she was extravagant. She spent hours at the bridge table, she had certain friends, cronies with whom she went on trips to health spas, to fashionable resorts . . .

By the time he was forty, and now fifty, he had had no sympathy whatever with her. The tall, thin woman in tailored slacks and jangling jewelry was as much a stranger to him as the tall, eyeglassed surgeon in the crowded o.r., demonstrating techniques, working with tiny babies that no other man would have tried to save, was to her.

Sometimes he thought about the "situation." In his thinking that night, listening to the wind moaning and creaking among the tall trees, Mac Webbe turned the word over and over in his mind. Yes, a situation it had been. Since he was thirty he had expected the time to come when he would want a woman of his own mental capacity.

Such women were available, others had offered themselves. And a time or two he had looked elsewhere. A handsome woman who had sat beside him on the plane when he was going to London for three weeks of teaching and learning. He had seen her constantly during those three weeks. He could have gone back, she might have come to him . . .

There was the redheaded young widow of a colleague. Webbe had found time and ways to comfort her in her loss, to help her reestablish her life. And scandal had circled about them for nearly a year; Elise had taunted him about it. "Maybe I should tell her what she would be getting!"

At the end of that year, his father had died. His mother had been dead for six years. And Webbe found himself settling and taking charge of a large estate. He was a rich man, though by then he was a rich man through his own work. He spent months seeing that his affairs were safely in order. His father's will had not mentioned either Elise or the children beyond leaving fifty dollars to each child. Though, of course, someday they might have a claim.

Mac gave the family mansion to the historical society, and with it nearly all of its richly significant furnishings. His father had traveled widely, he had served his country in various diplomatic and business ways, he had accumulated a store of mementoes, he had purchased art—

Elise had made a fine row over that gift. But she had never been welcome in his father's home; it must speak well for Mac's own attainments and performance that he had inherited the entire estate. And Elise's row—one more made no difference.

But then, at fifty, he was in a position, and the time had come, when he must decide what he was to do with the remaining years of his life. Professionally, the past thirty years had been creditable, and a bit more. Personally, they had been a wasteland—a desert of sand through which he had dutifully slogged his way.

Now . . .

He had seriously considered establishing and heading a foundation to research the care of birth-defect children. But in such a prestigious position, Elise would have made every effort to hold on to him. And time had shown that she was, and would be, of no help to him in the world of big medicine. He could think of occasions —once she had sat beside him at a banquet and had drunk too much—that had been embarrassing but harmed only those of sensitivity.

There had been the time when she had agreed to be interviewed by a ruthless man of the press. She had talked freely, and irresponsibly, about the politics involved in attaining the position which her husband now occupied.

That had done some real harm, to certain projects underway, to friendships, one of which Webbe deeply valued.

Now—

Now he had come to the mountains, to this place of quiet and safety, where the people seemed as large as their mountains, and where there was work to do.

Would Elise follow him here? Could she live here, endure the quiet pace and—well, if not help him, at least not hurt him, either? If not, there could be a divorce and a settlement.

He must see what could be done, in either direction.

Of course here, too, there promised to be Gretchen, and her not-too-subtle proffer. Could that young woman have guessed how vulnerable he was? He doubted it. He had long schooled himself to repress all personal things in his work, not ever revealing them to his fellow workers, or during any social encounters.

He did bitterly regret his too-early marriage. And resented the qualities within him that bound him to Elise. Though perhaps those things had also forced him into the great medical success he had known and his hoped-for determination as a man.

But, still, there was Elise. There was his wife.

And because of Elise, there were the three children. Now what would Miss Gretchen make of *them?*

Laughing softly, he stirred enough to extinguish the lantern, take off his boots, and crawl into his sleeping bag. He lay thinking about Gretchen. As lovely, as enchanting, as unpredictable as any child he had ever seen. And he had "seen" thousands of them.

And they were all alike. Gretchen was like them all. They could sit, these guileless creatures, in their high-chairs, faced with a cup of milk, a glass of fruit juice, a bowl of spinach and egg. They would lift one cup and eye Webbe warily, preparing to pour the whole mess together, but smiling winsomely, pretending they had no such intention.

Then, with concentration and lowered eyes, they would tip the cup gently, pleased when the cranberry juice turned the milk pink; the cup would overflow, and Webbe, or whoever, would only sit watching, and the child would regard the doctor with surprise. Then he would be ready to spank the whole mess together on the tray, and gleefully clash the cups together, garnishing the whole with glops of spinach.

Now and then he would tilt his head, puzzled, and ready to flirt appealingly. "Why don't you stop me? Don't you care?"

That was Gretchen. What would her sort do for a man, to a man? Even a man like McKinney Webbe?

Certainly Clancy Cobbins was a great guy.

What, really, was their marriage like? There were no children . . . And that was all he knew. So far.

Webbe fell asleep.

CHAPTER 10

He woke late the next morning, with the air icy against his cheek, his body warm in the down-filled bag. And some animal sniffing at his doorstep.

Groaning, he crawled out; he looked with distaste at the pans and the dishes left from last night, grease congealed in the fry pan, coffee cold in the pot. Could he get to the river for water to wash his face, to bring back to the camper? He tried to see the "animal," but the windows were high, and small. Curiously he opened the door at the front of the car. He could see nothing, and with some bravery, at which he smiled, he stepped out upon the frosty ground. Sunlight was marking the tops of the forest trees behind him, the arching sky was a tender blue. He went to the river, knelt beside it and gasped at the icy dash he scooped up for his face. He had brought no towel with him—a fine woodsman he was! He filled his bucket and hurried back to the camper.

Quickly he got it warm, and was even receptive to the idea of shaving after he had eaten the bacon and eggs and bread brought from the city. He peeled an orange, and changed his shirt.

What would he do next?

Wash up his dishes, and fish?

Or wash up his dishes, and drive farther into the mountains? He really did not want to fish, though he had been assured that the river was clear enough both for fishing and drinking.

He made things tidy and secure, then slid under the wheel. He had more thinking to do, and plans to make.

The road went up and around, and up again. It changed from cement to fine gravel, and narrowed. He slowed for three deer ahead of the car, smiling at the rosy pink which the sun showed through their lifted ears. He watched the road as he had been told, instead of the deep ravine which fell down, and down again from the side of the road. He kept his foot off the brake, accelerated cautiously, and came to a series of hairpin turns, and out upon what the map called a meadow.

And meadow it was, broad and sweet, with the snowy mountains rimming it, a distant farmhouse and large red barn, with cattle scattered across the fields, a pheasant flying picturesquely away from the encroaching car. Then, almost at once, it seemed, he was into the mountains again, with the forest coming down to the road on one side and "his" river thundering between its banks. Spray misted the windshield and the windows of the camper as the road followed closely beside the foaming white torrent of mountain water, boiling white over rocks, rising in great, surprising splashes. Beautiful, and fearsome, too.

He drove all morning, stopping at noon for sandwiches of the sausage and cheese which he had brought, and the can of tomato juice. He sat out on a sunny rock to eat, knowing that he must turn the wheels downward again toward home, his hospital, and his work. But for this hour he could think.

Just where had he stopped thinking the night before?

What a deep and restful sleep he had known!

He had been considering Elise—and remembering his children. He threw a crust of bread to an inquisitive ground squirrel, and stood up. Stretched his legs, and jogged in place for five minutes.

His children.

No longer that, of course. Ryder was twenty-nine, Tom was twenty-four, with Linda in between.

He sighed, policed the area, took his napkin, his tomato juice can and the knife back to the camper. He stowed the things neatly, promising himself to remove the litter bag when he reached the hospital that night.

And he sighed again as he got behind the wheel.

A man, he told himself solemnly, should never marry the wrong woman, if only because of the children. In his three children he had found the weaknesses they had inherited and learned from the mother which he had given them. They were born and grown to near teen-age, before that guilt had seized their father.

There was Linda. He had delighted in her birth. A father felt awe of his daughter, and delight. She had pale yellow hair, like silk clinging to a man's fingers, and solemn eyes, a true turquoise. She wheedled, she coaxed, she stole the things she wanted. An ice cream cone, a balloon—a pair of white shorts from a shop counter. Linda was lazy; her room was a cesspool. She was amoral. She seduced almost any boy or man, if not actually, then by intent. Then she lied and claimed that she could not walk along the street without some man propositioning her. This was not true, but scarcely anything she told was true. She was, the counselor told him, a congenital liar, like her mother. A psychological problem.

She lied to Mac, she lied to the teachers and deans of every school she attended; she lied to the police when she was caught shoplifting. She would agree to go to a psychiatrist, talk to a counselor—and sometimes she would go.

She left home, and returned—she said she was married. He suspected that she knew the drug scene, but he had shied away from proving the truth of this suspicion. The last thing he had done was to give her money to go to Mexico for a divorce from the man she claimed had forced her to marry him. She was tall, like Elise, with blond hair, which she bleached white, and a figure of which she was proud. She ate poorly, smoked constantly—and unless she changed, her habits would catch up with her.

Yes, he loved her. Rather, he loved what she might have been.

Then there was Tom.

A slender, dark-haired man. As he had been a slender, dark-haired little boy, mischievous, naughty, stubborn. Elise said he was just like her brother, and he was. That brother had deserted from the army, and the family had not heard from him in years. Tom—he was short in a family of tall people. Short in schools that placed a premium on size. He could not make any team except tennis. And making teams was the goal of his life.

As an adult, he was insecure, and concealed it by outrageous behavior. He talked a lot, blustered and bragged. He did not finish at college, and refused to return and try again. He continued to play tennis, but was not as good at it as he claimed.

He had one talent. Of making what his exasperated father called a jackass of himself in public, at social affairs. Which was embarrassing, but could be endured.

When Tom was twenty, he was arrested for forging a check with his father's name. Dr. Webbe would not press charges. But thereafter he watched the boy very closely. He caught him promoting something he called a deal among Webbe's professional colleagues. And he was shocked, angered, ashamed. He also stopped things in time, his action resulting in a bruising row with Elise. She never had understood discipline, that of his parents, nor that which Mac had tried to show to his children.

Then, this past year, Tom had asked his father, brashly, for a large sum of money. He had a land deal he could buy into, and of course his "old man" was loaded. When Mac refused, Tom promised to blackmail him, to give interviews to the newspaper, to involve the whole family and certain friends. His mother and Linda had promised to help him get some cash from the estate.

It was that development, and the legal steps which he had to take, that made Webbe decide to change his whole life, to walk out on his medical position, which he would not have hurt, and his family, who stood ready to hurt him. He would leave his broken home and his medical eminence and start over in some place small enough, quiet enough . . .

This was not the first thinking he had done on the subject. These were not the first questions he had asked.

But he felt that no man should ask himself to be struck time and time again by shame and failure in his personal life. How long could he protect his professional standing against these attacks upon him? And he asked himself if his professional life might be the cause of his children's weakness, their failure?

He was at fault, surely, to some degree. The sort of man he was, to work hard, to be uncompromising, the sort of woman Elise was— Both parents were at fault; they always were—both for what they had done, and had not done, for their children. Of course, if that were true, Mac must give some credit to Elise for Ryder.

And he would. Because there was enough good in Ryder that he could afford to let Elise have some of the award.

Midafternoon, he stopped and went into a roadside café for coffee and to stretch his limbs.

Had he accomplished anything at all by his journey into the forest? Fresh air in his lungs, a need to look up at the mountains and the trees, the memory of swift, cold waters—they must help a man, and turn his thinking forward rather than—

He had considered divorce as one solution of his troubles with Elise. He had considered that step often before.

But now, if he considered it, if he actually did divorce Elise, and remarried, could he not, would he not repeat all the mistakes already made?

And what about Elise? He wondered about her life. She probably could tell her side of their marriage, and make a brief as impressive as his own. She could cite his lack of understanding, his absorption in his work to the abandonment of his home and family, his unwillingness to forgive, or understand, what she called human mistakes . . .

She would claim her rights, and no doubt she had some.

But so did Mac. So did he.

After another hour the lights of the valley began to shine dimly below him. Up where he was, there still was sunshine.

He found himself looking forward to reaching "home." To go into the hospital, up to his room, to shower and change, and make rounds—eat dinner. Not rested, perhaps, but relieved in many ways.

He had decided almost nothing about himself and his problems. About all he had done was to relive a portion of his life. Some of it, that part so intimately concerned with his children, seemed to be new to him, as if he had not shared those times.

But he did think he had defined his problems, set them up in a line. From there he could move . . .

When he returned the camper to Jim Adams, he told his new friend that he had enjoyed the trip.

"Did you go alone?" asked Jim casually.

"Well, of course."

Jim's eyebrows went up. "Not too good an idea in these mountains," he said. "Or anywhere else, I imagine. And I can think of several willing companions you might have invited."

"Next time, give me your list at the beginning of my expedition," Mac retorted.

"Make one of your own. It probably would be better and longer."

The idea was intriguing and Webbe toyed with it for his own amusement. He was making friends . . .

The Cobbinses and the Pursers, the Adamses, and Jonah IntVeld, Til Holt. Some of the hospital people. Susan Warrington. She had been a guest at Gretchen's dinner party.

And he encountered her again when she came to work as a volunteer at the well-baby clinic, which he had set up, with Gretchen in charge.

She spoke of the young woman as "Clancy's girl friend," so explanations were in order. Susan had laughed at her impudence. "I pay Clancy for all the time he gives me," she assured the tall Chief of Staff.

"And Gretchen spends the money," Dr. Webbe concluded.

Gretchen nodded. "You bet I do."

"He's a beautiful man," Gretchen told Susan when Dr. Webbe had left them. "He does some wonderful things for the kids in this ward."

"I thought he was a surgeon."

"He is. And he does a full schedule of surgery three or four days a week. He runs the hospital Medical Service, and still finds time to give to the kids. He's been here three months, and the things he's done . . ." She broke off to weigh a curly-haired baby. She called him Pedro, though that was not his name. "All Chicanos are Pedro," she had assured Susan. "I like working in the well-baby clinic. But—"

Her vivid face sobered. "We have other babies—hospital patients—that are not well. Some are—" She broke off, and shook her head.

Susan watched her. "Gretch," she asked, "why don't you have some babies of your own?"

"I shall, someday," said Gretchen.

"Time gets away from a girl, you know."

"Yes. Do you wish that you and Tony . . . ?"

"Yes, I do. But he thought he was too old. He knew he would not live to raise a child."

"You could find yourself another man, Sue. There are several."

"Your Dr. Webbe, for one?" laughed Susan, taking the baby and beginning to dress him.

Gretchen wrote things on the chart. "Didn't you know," she asked, "that Webbe is married?"

"This child has three arms!" gasped Susan, struggling with a small undershirt and a busy baby. "No, I didn't know. Where is she? His wife?"

Gretchen shrugged. "She had better be here, keeping an eye on him," she said.

They were finished with Pedro, and Susan undressed the next baby, a tiny one whose mother insisted on coming into the examining room.

"Is Dr. Webbe still on the floor?" Gretchen asked Susan, her tone quiet.

"Do you need him?"

"If he's close . . ." She merely glanced at the telephone, but Susan was learning fast.

Dr. Webbe came in at once. "What do we have here?" he asked, breezing in, his eyeglasses sparkling, his coattails flying.

"My baby don't eat," said the mother anxiously.

"She came to the wrong clinic," said Gretchen. "It's her first visit."

The Chief's hands and eyes moved swiftly. "I think

you're right, Doctor," he said. "There's at least a bad hernia here. Mrs. Warrington, will you wrap the baby, just in the blanket, and take him up to surgery? I'll talk to the mother, and be right there. Tell the nurse—"

Susan stared at Gretchen. "What do I do now?" she asked faintly.

"Do what the doctor says, darling. Surgery is two floors up. Just repeat what he said. The baby's insides are in a bad shape. And I'm stuck with well-baby, though I do love to watch that man operate."

"On a baby that little?" asked Susan.

"Get going!" said Gretchen.

When Susan came back, she made Gretchen talk to her. Gretchen was working on a boy of four who needed a bath. "But under all that dirt he's healthy!" said the doctor.

"Tell me about that baby upstairs, and about Dr. Webbe!" Sue insisted.

"I'm going to. Take off this kid's shoes, will you? Then he can't—do—so—much damage—when he kicks."

But between patients, she did talk to Susan about Dr. Webbe. "In a lot of books in the hospital library," she said, "you can read about the techniques he's developed. I don't know why he gave all that up to come out here and be our Chief of Staff and do general surgery. He's good at that, too, but— And he still loves the children most. Why— Well, I'll tell you about Margaret."

"Margaret who?" asked Susan.

Gretchen brushed her hair back from her face. "What difference does that make?"

"I don't know. I just asked."

"Yes, you did. Well, when Webbe first came here, we

had Margaret in the ward. Giamonco said she had nephritis, and he had told the parents that she would die."

"Did she? How old was she?"

"She was sixteen months old, and children with nephritis often do die. The doctors don't know much about it. But when Webbe showed up and examined her, he asked me if I knew any children with the measles."

"Measles!"

"Yes, it does sound crazy. But the books agreed with him. Getting measles does help these kids. Doctors don't know why about that, either. Anyway—I found a child, Margaret played with him. And did not catch the measles.

"We found another case. Same thing. No measles for Margaret. And Mac—I mean Dr. Webbe—began to think of what else he could do for the little girl. She was a sweet child. Then, guess what? They let her go home for the weekend, and she played with some visiting cousins. And, of course, one of them was coming down with the measles. So did Margaret. And sure enough, she is improving in the kidney department, too."

"Kidney . . . ?"

Gretchen laughed merrily. "Oh, Susan!" she cried. "You really don't know nuthin' about medicine, do you?"

"I don't pretend to, but I'll admit that Dr. Webbe does sound wonderful!"

"I tried to say he was, about Margaret, but you should have heard him explain that Margaret, without him, but with the cousin to play with, would be right where she is if he had stayed on the East Coast."

"I'm glad he didn't," said Susan firmly.

"We are all glad. But he's that way, works hard, does fine things, and is afraid to make close friends. Are we through with the babies?"

"There aren't any more in the hall."

"Well, glory be! Let's wash up and get some coffee. We'll detour through surgery to see how the baby with the scrambled guts is doing. My, that must have been a mess!"

"How old . . . ?"

"Two weeks."

"Why didn't the obstetrician see that things were wrong?"

Gretchen glanced at her. "What obstetrician?" she asked.

"You mean . . . ?"

"Didn't you know?" Gretchen asked. "Babies are born under cabbage leaves. And if their insides are popping out of their navels, it's a blessed thing that Dr. Webbe came to Idaho."

Dr. Webbe, coming on the floor, overheard this, and he stood watching the young women going down the hall, Gretchen laughing happily at something or other. He nodded to himself. He probably had discovered the right place for Gretchen to work. If she continued to work. A girl like that should have her own babies. Clancy's, or those of some other lucky man. Life with Gretchen would be a wonderful thing.

He shook his head and sternly rebuked his errant thoughts. Surely there was work enough to do in this fine, clean hospital to keep him busy. He'd better get about doing that work.

And he did get about it.

CHAPTER 11

SPRING came early to the mountain valley. With snow still shoulder-high beside the roads "up hill," and the flashlights and torches of skiers still to be watched in the cold dark of evening, jonquils bloomed in the dooryards on the valley floor. And Dr. Webbe set about making the changes he wanted in the hospital. He asked for, and got from the Board, permission to do the necessary things to tighten the staff. He dismissed no one, but rigidly set up patterns for duty and behavior. The new internist came, another M.D., and Dr. Fielder decided that he was getting too old to work as hard and as steadily as "that new fella" seemed to require.

Dr. Webbe agreed that the old man should take a well-earned rest. "We'll call on you as we need you, sir," he said courteously.

He arranged, until they could get a full-time man, to have a pathologist and a certified radiologist come up from Salt Lake City two days a week. These, Mondays and Thursdays for the radiologist, became rat races for doctors and their patients needing tests and examinations.

Tissue meetings must be held, and were held. Webbe had set up every needed hospital-service committee, and he attended their meetings, sternly demanding full and quick reports on them. He called on the carpet anyone guilty of bad medicine. A surgeon, opening an abdomen to take out a healthy appendix, had to be able to talk fast and to the point. And still would probably have his surgery restricted.

Records meetings were held once a month. The charts of doctors, nurses and lab workers were considered. Any one of them not fully completed must be completed.

Gretchen, for one, admired what the new Chief was doing. "But I'd think he would fall to pieces at his bedtime," she told Clancy. "Whenever that is. I know the rest of us collapse."

"But you like it?"

"I like going on a roundup with Dad, but when I get home again, I sleep for a week."

"Your dad has asked Webbe to come along when they move the cattle."

"Oh, I'll go too!"

"Wait until you're asked, maybe?"

"Oh . . ."

"Won't he expect you to take care of things down here? At the hospital, I mean."

"I suppose so. He thinks he's making a pediatrician out of me."

"Let him. You'll like it."

"I like . . ."

"I know. But this time I'll go on the roundup, you stay down here and imagine the sort and size of rock we'll have under our respective sleeping bags."

But of course Gretchen still wanted to go; she loved these expeditions, and was a real help. But she wanted to please Dr. Webbe, too. Though she could have helped him enjoy the drive. Could he ride a horse? she wondered. Would he stand picket duty? Would he take care of his precious hands?

Dr. Webbe enjoyed the three-day expedition. He stood picket duty, and he did take care of his hands. Hugh Purser gave him the needed leather gloves. "You'll be saddle-sore, Doctor."

"I expect to be. And the hospital will expect me to waddle like a duck when I return."

Hugh Purser laughed. "Well, have fun . . ."

Mac would always tell how he enjoyed those three days, beginning with the roundup of the cattle, and the drive upward, the dashes to head off a wandering cow or steer, the hearty meals at dawn and at sunset, and the four hours he spent in the moonlight, patrolling the picket line, watchful that the animals grazed quietly and together, that no marauder threatened.

That was the best. The cold mountain air, washed silver by moonlight. It steamed from his lips; he sucked it into his lungs with genuine pleasure.

"Marlboro country," he told himself sardonically. "I should sing . . ."

And scare the wits out of man and beast alike.

"How Ryder would love this," he thought. Ryder. In his thoughts about himself, his past, and his family, now was the time to think about his third child, his oldest child. Ryder. A doctor, doing well in orthopedic surgery. Almost thirty years old, and Webbe's son, entirely.

* * *

Webbe had not spoiled him. He had not! In fact, he had given more time, and certainly had spent more money, on the other two. But Ryder had never given him one minute of worry. And one came to appreciate that. The pride and love which Tom and Linda rejected as unneeded, Webbe had been able to feel in full for his tall, blond son.

To have such a son was more than many men ever got out of life.

With his thoughts so much on Ryder, it did not surprise him too much to find that young man at the hospital, waiting for his father when he returned, dirty, tired, yes, and saddle'-sore, on the night of the roundup's third day.

"I expected you to go western," drawled the younger doctor, "but this is ridiculous!"

Mac grinned and ran the brim of his Stetson through his fingers. "How did you persuade them to let you into my room?"

"There was this handsome blonde . . ."

"Oh, oh," said Mac.

"She said you'd hired out as a hand to her father."

"I had. All the beans, skillet biscuits and inch-thick steaks I could eat."

"You look great, Dad."

"So do you."

Ryder grinned. "You must know this blonde."

"What did she say?"

"Well—she's a bit introverted."

"For the mountains, maybe. I had a cow push me

down over a five-foot cliff day before yesterday, horse and all."

"Uh-huh. Well, when I gave this blonde my name, she said—and remember, I'm quoting—she said, 'Oh, gorgeous!' "

Mac laughed. "You're bragging."

"Yeah. And then she said I was just like you, and that you knew how much she loved you."

Mac laughed aloud, and Ryder joined him. "I'll have to find a bed for you," Dr. Webbe said. "You certainly can't have mine. Not tonight."

"No. I'll go to the hotel."

"Not unless this hospital is more full than it was when I left."

"Can you put me in a maternity ward bed without permission of the State Board of Health? We can't do that in Missouri."

"Sounds like a good law. Maybe we should both work in Missouri."

"I believe you like Idaho. Lordy, what a sunburn!"

"Sun, snow, and wind burn. I'll shower . . ."

"Don't sing."

"I won't. It panicked the herd, too."

The next day, Ryder accompanied his father on hospital rounds. And of course they came upon Gretchen.

"Well, well," she said. "That's a fine son you have there, Doctor. Could be he might put you out of first place."

"It could be," said Dr. Webbe. "He usually does."

Gretchen smiled. "How were the mountains?" she asked.

"Rocky. Rocky all over."

"Clancy said they were. I figured he was getting old and soft."

"No, the rocks were hard, and sharp. You seem to have managed well here, Doctor."

"For you I can do anything," said Gretchen demurely.

Smiling, the two tall men continued on their way, from bed to bed, alert and interested. Ryder was slender and, though blond, like his father in a dozen ways. His features were softer, perhaps; he wore no glasses, and of course he was younger; his eyes were inquiring of everything; Mac read some things at a glance.

The men finished that area and progressed to another. In the elevator, Ryder asked, "Is she serious, Dad?"

His father glanced at him.

"Your new pediatrician."

"Oh! Oh, yes, she could be serious."

Ryder shook his head. "Are you worried?"

"About her? No, I'm not worried."

His son looked at him, concern beginning to darken his own eyes.

"Look," said Mac, holding the elevator at the floor, turning to face his son. "I read her as a girl who had been popular all her life. She has always been ready to snag the new boy . . ."

"You can't mean me!"

"My reign has been short." He stepped out of the elevator.

Ryder started to follow him to the chart desk, then he turned. "You can't be serious!"

"I could be," said Mac.

"Well—I'll say this. She is quite a dish."

"Oh, yes. And with brains, as well."

"That's a bad combination. You'd better watch it, sir."

Dr. Webbe asked the floor nurse for the charts. "All the time," he said to his son. "All the time."

Back in St. Louis, Ryder had a good practice and hospital staff affiliations, but he stayed with his father for all of that week, even doing some surgery with him. Gretchen said, in a staff meeting, that it was not necessary to identify which Dr. Webbe was speaking or doing. "You need only to look to see the father in the son."

The other doctors laughed politely, but the statement clung to Mac's mind and thoughts. For him, it was like seeing another chance presented.

And he began to cherish the idea that the two men could make a life together. One of pride, and good work, and—

Did Ryder fully know his father's problems? Or about his mistakes?

Could he tell his son about them, and about the problems still facing him?

As happened occasionally, the question was answered for him. He had spoken to Ryder about finding a small house, or an apartment for him, away from the hospital. Ryder agreed that this would be advisable. "Since you are increasing your staff, you won't need to be house doctor around the clock. And you should qualify for intern service in another year."

"I plan to try."

They looked at the small, pleasant house which had been recommended to Dr. Webbe. It was a low ranch-style, set back into a small grove of conifers. There was a fireplace, and a place where a swimming pool could be built.

"The essentials in any man's life," Ryder agreed. "Are you going to be your own cook?"

"I can be, if necessary. Or eat at the hospital. I'll certainly need furniture, and to get myself decorated."

"What about the row house in Maryland?"

Mac shrugged. "Your mother is living there, I suppose."

"Don't you know?"

"I get bills."

"That's a good clue. Dad . . ."

Mac turned to look at his son. "Yes?" he asked.

"I want to get this said. Though it may not need saying."

Mac waited.

"I wanted you to know that I fully understood why you left. I know there has been no divorce, though there probably should be one. In any case, I also admire the way you've stuck with Mother. I know she . . ."

Dr. Webbe lifted his hand, palm flat. "Wait a minute," he said. "Let's get one thing straight. I've been sticking with the *family.*"

"Yes," said Ryder. "Yes, you have."

"I had my problems. I still have them. They show up as regularly as the light and phone bills. And they probably will continue to do that. But I have managed to do one thing."

"Now?" asked Ryder, in surprise.

"Yep. Now. Now—here—I can work. And figure out a way to live my life."

Ryder laughed. "And you think all you need is a swimming pool."

"I do. Picture how popular I shall be if I have one."

An hour later, when they entered the main lobby of the hospital, he said under his breath that he should have bitten his tongue.

For slumped into one of the deep chairs was his daughter Linda, a suitcase beside the chair.

CHAPTER 12

"I'LL HAVE to buy that house," he told Ryder later that week.

"With all your problems sitting on your roof?"

"I was crazy to expect anything else. How long are you staying?"

"I can manage the rest of this month. Long enough to get the place livable for you, or do anything else I can to help."

"I shan't ask too much. And the place is small. Two bedrooms. That limits things."

"There's a den. And if we put a couch in the living room . . ." Ryder was smiling.

"I can always sleep at the hospital."

"Did Linda talk to you?"

"Yes. She said Tom had been arrested again. For forgery."

"What did you promise to do?"

"Nothing."

"Dad . . . ?"

"Look, son, you're new at this thing. I have already

made *that* mistake. I bailed him out. I took the punishment. Now it's his turn. I feel for the prison authorities, but two years in prison may be what that young man needs."

"You won't sleep nights."

"Maybe *you* won't. And maybe I'll lie awake some, feeling guilty. But at least I shan't be wondering what Tom will do next. For two years, I'll know!"

Ryder shrugged. "Did you tell Linda that?"

"I did. And she promised to get even with me."

"How?"

"I don't know. She could talk to the newspapers, perhaps. Man of wealth lets son go to jail for forgery."

"Mhmmnn. Opinion might split right up the middle on that. And, since you asked me, have you asked Linda how long *she* is going to stay around here?"

"No. I have not. She seems to be enjoying herself. Gretchen is being what she considers nice to her."

"Yes. And Linda is making eyes at Gretchen's husband. I've seen it."

"Clancy is nobody's fool."

But, without being a fool, Clancy could be put into a bad position.

Gretchen was the first to tell Webbe about it. She had arranged a Sunday picnic and all-day party up at Lucky Peak Lake, and she had asked Til Holt to be Linda Webbe's escort. He had not especially wanted to do this.

"Why not?" Gretchen asked him.

"Let her brother take her."

"What girl wants to go to parties with her *brother?*"

"Maybe not Linda," Til agreed, grinning. "But why

do we have to have escorts? Aren't Mac and Ryder both invited?"

"Yes. But Mac is on call. And Ryder said only *maybe.*"

"I like him better than I do Linda."

"Oh, Til."

"I think Miss Linda knows that."

"And she probably did know it," said Gretchen when she brought her story to Linda's father. As she did on the afternoon following the picnic. Mac and Ryder had spent the morning in o.r. together. Then Ryder had gone out to the house to see how the swimming pool was coming along.

And Gretchen . . .

"She has a way of complicating things," thought Dr. Webbe as he listened to her story. And made notes. He wrote that thought down, too.

"You should have come to my party," said Gretchen accusingly. "And Til should have pretended that he was delighted to take Linda."

"Tell me what happened, what's been done," said Dr. Webbe patiently.

"I thought I had told you."

"Not reasonably, nor quietly. And not at all in sequence."

Gretchen paced around his office. "A lot of nasty people are going to be pleased about this," she said. "Shaw, and Kathy—"

"Kathy Binnard? Was she at the party?"

"No, of course not. She's as big as a hippo with that baby she shouldn't be having. But she will be glad to see Til on the spit, whether he deserves to be or not."

"Gretchen, are you going to tell me your story?"

"I know. Reasonably. From the first. Well, there was the party. A very nice one, with the usual high jinks and stuff. Good food, water skiing—some drinking, but not too much. People starting their suntans, and Linda in a string bikini that was out of this world, though Til told her she didn't have the proper *derrière* for it, and that made her mad."

Dr. Webbe laughed.

"I don't know whether they made up or not. If her story is true, they must have—"

Dr. Webbe waited.

"Well, anyway," Gretchen continued. "She came to Clancy's office this morning . . ."

"Linda did? By herself?"

"Yes, she said she thought she ought to have a lawyer before she went to the police with her complaint." Gretchen looked expectantly at the chief. "You didn't know about this?"

"Not a word."

"Well, Clancy says she evidently didn't know that he's acting Prosecuting Attorney for the county since the other man died last month. Just until election next fall."

"I didn't know that, either."

"Now Clancy thinks that maybe she did know, but pretended not to. Anyway, she said she wanted him to represent her, and file charges—"

And further implicate the hospital and embarrass me, thought Linda's father. To pay me off for not helping Tom.

"Clancy asked me to explain his position to you," said Gretchen after a minute. "He supposed you knew the story, and said that normally he would want to help you.

He likes you, Doctor."

"I like Clancy. Now, suppose you tell me the story."

Gretchen marveled at the poise of the man. He must be disturbed, but he displayed nothing except quiet interest.

"Well," she said slowly, "Linda claims that Til Holt, the City Manager, raped her at my party."

"Oh, Gretchen!"

"I have my own ideas of rape charges," Gretchen agreed. "Especially at parties like that one. String bikinis, and all."

"And it takes two to tango," said Mac Webbe dryly.

"But she's gone to the police, and told the newspaper. Claims she was a virgin . . ."

That broke his composure. Dr. Webbe was out of his chair. "The woman's been married!" he shouted. "I'll talk to Clancy about this!" He turned and confronted Gretchen, his face white and stern. "Did Clancy ask you to tell me all this?" he demanded.

"No, he didn't. But he did seem relieved when I said I was going to do it. Of course he knows that I am crazy about you."

"Oh, *Gretchen!*"

"This is all off the ethical record," she said calmly. "I'm crazy about Ryder, too. But that daughter of yours . . . Clancy didn't want me to give that party for her."

"Why did you?"

"To please you."

"Well, you were badly off target!" He sat down again at his desk. "When did Linda see Clancy?"

"This morning. It must have been early. A little before twelve he came here and ate lunch with me. He was considerably upset. He has to file the charges. Had to. And since Til is City Manager—he's a good one!—the City Council had a hurry-up meeting in special session, and requested Til's suspension pending the outcome of the criminal charges. They named the Public Works director manager for the time."

"Where's Til?"

"He's out on bail, or recognizance, or something. Nobody thinks your daughter was hurt. But of course the newspaper and the radio have the story. All about the party and—everything. The town will have a field day. I can just hear Ida B. and Kathy—"

Dr. Webbe sat thoughtful, then he reached for the telephone. "I want to talk to Clancy," he told Gretchen. "This is not a nice thing."

"Not very, no," Gretchen agreed.

He did talk to Clancy, and Gretchen listened, shooing off his secretary who tried, once, to come into the office.

Finally he put the phone down, and put his head in his hands. "I have to go see Linda," he said wearily.

"What did Clancy say?"

"That I should get her to withdraw her charges. She has no case. *I* say she will have to leave town."

"Will she expect you to pay her to do this?"

"If so, she is due for a disappointment. I have told my family that they are on their own. With a couple of them, this doesn't set well. What concerns me is: how can we make this up to Holt?"

"He must be angry, but he won't sue Linda."

"He won't do anything to Linda, but it is going to be hell to do his job. If the Council lets him keep his job."

"They'd better!" said Gretchen grimly.

"You're to stay out of this, Gretchen."

"I know. Clancy told me the same thing."

"Listen to him! As for Til, he'll have enough to handle. His enemies will seek to make something out of this mess."

"I don't think he has many enemies. He's a nice guy."

Dr. Webbe stood up slowly, as if he were very weary. "I'm a nice guy, too," he said. "And I have enemies."

"Where are you going?"

"To check on my post-ops, then to find Ryder, then we'll both find Linda . . ." He left the office.

And why, he was to ask before that week was done, *why* did his whole family—his whole *damn* family!—descend on him at once?

"I'm going to ask Clancy," he told Ryder, "if a man can divorce his family."

"He'll tell you that he can, if he survives their coming of age."

"I know. That's the law of it. But there are ties. Fathers have umbilical cords too, you know."

"I know." Ryder's eyes were somber with his thoughts.

"Now this thing about your mother . . ."

"There's a funny side to that, Dad."

"I'm glad you can see it," said Mac grimly. They were at the new house. All furnished and "decorated," an attractive place. The pool was built, and filled; it needed some planting, some chairs and tables—but Mac had his home.

"It is funny," Ryder insisted, rattling the ice in his glass. "Here you think you are ready to set up housekeeping as a bachelor and— Have you talked to

Clancy about a divorce?"

"Not yet. I'm beginning to sympathize with patients who don't bring their V.D. or their cancerous lung to the doctor. Lawyers are discreet, they are kind, but who wants to share some secrets with an outsider?"

"I know, Dad. But they tracked you down . . ."

"Your mother had my address."

"Of course she did. But you didn't keep in touch. You didn't know she was traveling in Greece or Lithuania, or wherever it was. But the telephone connection was made — Did you talk to Mother?"

"Oh, no. The man—from the Embassy, he said. He said she was on her way home. That this country—the State Department—since they had had some problems before—had decided that it was best for all concerned to cancel her passport."

"I see. Because she had made some trouble."

"Legal trouble, he said. Just as Linda did here."

"Well, Mother and Linda do think alike."

"Yes, I'm afraid they do. They lie, they— This time she was telling that she was being persecuted."

"In what way?"

"I didn't ask. This courteous man was just saying that her passport had been lifted, and he wanted me to know why. He also wanted to tell me that she was on her way home."

"He hoped."

"Without a passport, she had better be!"

"Yes, of course. Does she know that you are living out here? I mean, planning to live here?"

"She knows where I am. I suppose she'll keep the old residence."

"She may not."

"Then she can come here. Though she likes to travel."

Both men laughed. "I'll be hearing from her," Mac said.

And now father and son were counting the days until Ryder would have to leave. "I've stalled all I can," he told his father.

"I can put you to work, as of tomorrow."

"For now, you've had a big dose of family."

"But the wrong kind of medicine."

"Yes. Was the Binnard baby born today?"

"It was. It won't live. I hope. When I first came here, we tried to talk that mother into an abortion. Her husband had religious scruples, but he consented. That is, he gave the decision to his wife."

"An alcoholic."

"That's right. I predicted the baby would have birth defects, die, or have a low mental capacity. Incidentally, he's still being stubborn, that father."

"Gretchen tells me they are friends. She and the mother, I mean. Girl friends."

"That's true. But Gretchen didn't have any luck telling her what to do. Though, of course, without the husband's consent, we would not have aborted. Now—the child won't live."

"And the mother?"

"She may change. She probably won't stay with Binnard. There's gossip that she married him because Til Holt wouldn't marry her."

"Holt again."

"He's a good man. He was right not to want an alcoholic wife. I wish Kathy could be made to see how right he was."

"Everybody has his troubles," said Ryder, then glanced at his father. "I'm allowed one platitude a day?"

"Or two . . ." Webbe was thinking deeply.

"Gretchen might be the very one to turn Kathy around. She told me today that she was sorry your daughter had caused trouble for you. She said you were a wonderful man, and should have a good and peaceful life, instead of such hellish things happening to you."

"Mhmmmn," murmured Mac. Ryder thought his father was about to fall asleep. He was not. He was thinking. Only that afternoon, Gretchen had listened to his argument for helping Kathy, and had said that she might not be available.

"I think I may offer to go back with Ryder," she had said.

"Why do you say that?" Meaning, why would she think Ryder would allow her to—

"I need to know more about medicine. He is on staff in a big teaching hospital. We could work together."

"What about me?" he had asked. "And what about Clancy?" He didn't remember what answer she'd thought up. He was asking himself, "What about the boy? What about Ryder?"

He had been completely dismayed by her announcement. If she carried out her plan, she could ruin his "boy"! And what should his father do to intervene? For he must do something!

CHAPTER 13

And then, again, he found that he need do nothing.

Because Clancy Cobbins stepped in. Mac should have known that such a smart young man would not have been blind to what Gretchen was doing, and wildly planning. He was a good lawyer, and Webbe was planning to place his own tangled affairs into his hands. Clancy had helped him with Linda, and he would be equally quiet and knowing about the other family situations. Divorce, a new will to make, and—

It was Clancy who asked for a chance to talk to Dr. Webbe. "At your convenience, sir. Any hour, anytime—"

"Has something else come up, Clancy? You yourself are not ill?"

"Oh, nothing of that sort. I would just like to get some things straightened out."

"Well, I have some tangles of my own. Would you like to come out to my new home this afternoon? Late? I think we could be undisturbed there."

It was arranged. Clancy was there by five, and inspected the place with interest. "You have a good view," he said with satisfaction.

"I do. Sawtooths from the patio, Oregon mountains from the front windows. Obscured some mornings, but they are there!"

"They always have been."

"Of course I don't have Gretchen's mountain in my back yard."

Clancy had accepted a long chair, and stretched out on it. Now he sat erect and leaned toward his host. "It's Gretchen I came here to talk about," he said earnestly.

"Before or after a drink?"

"I'll state my problems, then we can have a drink, and after that, you can tell me about your tangles."

"That sounds like a good plan." Mac sat quietly in his own chair. He's not a man to relax, thought Clancy.

"Well, mine's a request, sir," he said. Then he sat thoughtful for a minute. "Before you actually came to our hospital, but after I had told her you were coming, Gretchen and I made a compact between us. It had to do with her medical career. I knew she was restless. She had got her M.D. but she had not done internships, or opened an office. It seemed to me that she was just playing with being a doctor. She did some things, but without any real dedication to the profession. For a couple of years she was engrossed in building the house. But keeping house is no career to hold her interest. She wasn't ready to have a family—so I was pleased when she consented to work steadily with you. There had been an occurrence in the hospital which convinced her that she needed more training."

"She has worked, Clancy. I don't know about the dedication . . ."

"I don't think she herself feels that she is dedicated. But I do think if you would keep her to her teaching-learning relationship, it would help. Lately, she's gone off on a tangent or two . . ."

"I'll do what I can, Clancy. I have been interested in working with Gretchen, amused often by her, but I have made plans. They did not include what she came up with today, but—"

Clancy's head lifted. "Now what?"

"Well, she'll tell you. So I may as well do it, too. She said today that she thought she wanted to work in a large teaching hospital."

"Why that? She did her medical school work in such a place, and didn't even apply for an internship. She could have stayed there . . ."

Mac frowned. "I don't think so, Clancy. I know none of the details, but something happened that made her run for home and clear away from medicine for a time."

Clancy thought about this. Then he looked up again. "Does she want to go where Ryder is?" he asked quietly.

Dr. Webbe stood up. "I'm going to get us that drink," he said. "Your immediate problem is solved. Ryder will be back here in six months, and we'll both stand ready to teach Miss Gretchen. If, by then, that is what she wants."

He went into the house, leaving a very puzzled young husband to watch the changing colors of the evening sky.

"Now!" he said when he returned, pushing a small, wheeled cart that held ice and supplies for their drinks, a covered wedge of cheese and some crackers.

"My problems will take much longer," he explained. "I want my attorney well-fed and alert."

"Your attorney," said Clancy dryly.

"Yes. I'll make it official later, but I thought right at first a sidewalk consultation would do."

He did have things to say. For a self-contained man, Webbe was keyed up about something.

Clancy waited, getting excited himself, he found, as the doctor talked.

He had first to confess, Webbe said, that he was a wealthy man. "Stinking rich, actually," he added, as if that was something to confess. No, not rich from his profession, though that bank account was exceedingly healthy. Then he told about his father, and his grandfather—"I did not want to enter their business. And they let me do what I did want to do, assuring themselves, and me, that medicine was what I wanted."

The business had thrived, and expanded, and, in his father's later years—"he was sixty"—it had been sold for a great sum of money. "Since it was a family project, that great sum descended on me when my parents died. Not to my children, you understand, but to me. There were a few simple bequests, but there I was, a surgeon suddenly damn rich." He mentioned a figure which brought Clancy upright again.

"Good Lord, Doc!" he breathed.

"Yes. And there I was, with the family I had. Ryder is okay. I would trust him with anything. You've met Linda, too, and she would indicate that I was not interested in spreading the wealth. So! What I am going to do, what I want to do, Clancy, is to establish a foundation. For a time I avoided that solution, but now I want to do what is necessary to establish a hospital, a research center, to care for babies with birth defects."

"And you'll head this? You'll be leaving us."

"No. No, I won't. Because I have fallen deeply in love with this country, the clear air, the water, the people, the views of sky and water and tall trees . . ."

"And desert and sagebrush," drawled Clancy, but his eyes were shining. "A research foundation here?" he asked. "Right *here*, Mac?"

"Well, not on this patio. But if we can keep the project quiet—I'm businessman enough not to want to be *done*. I thought something near the hospital—if we can get land—"

"Our hospital?"

"Yes. Your hospital. The Board would have to agree and cooperate . . ."

Clancy was on his feet. He walked around the pool, and looked for a minute as if he were about to plunge into it. He was talking to himself.

"I call the project, in my mind," said Mac quietly, "the Kathy Binnard Clinic."

"The . . . ?" Clancy turned sharply.

"It's for sad little creatures like her baby."

"Ryder told me about that." He came swiftly back to where Dr. Webbe sat. "What about Ryder?" he asked. "Does he have a hand in this?"

"Yes, he does. He is the one good apple on my family tree, Clancy. He and I will work on this together. I have built my reputation on infant surgical techniques. Ryder is a fine young surgeon. There is money enough . . . if carefully managed. We can even take mothers like Kathy and perhaps begin to help the fetal child."

Clancy was gazing at him in awe. "You do think *big!*" he said. "We thought we were doing a big thing to get you as Chief of Staff for our hospital."

"You did. Big for me, as well, and for my family, though they won't appreciate that placing all that money into a trust that they, and I, can't touch, will eventually help them. Ryder does. He says he can guess at the load lifted from me, because of his own relief."

"And he's coming back here."

"Yes."

"Wait until Gretchen hears this! She'll have a lot of things to learn right here."

"There will be dozens of details to work out before we can even announce the foundation. The property, laws — Oh, you will be a busy man!"

"Me? I'm just a mountain lawyer."

"You're my attorney. You'll learn what you need to learn, just as Ryder and I shall. Meanwhile, he'll go on our present hospital staff, and we'll eventually find and bring in new men, a new chief."

"You're sneaky, too," said Clancy admiringly. "One of the dozens of details I'll have to handle will be trouble from the rest of your family."

"Probably. They'll call me incompetent, and many other nasty things."

"While the foundation is still a secret, we'll make it family-proof, if that is what you really want."

"Sometime—not tonight—I'll let my hair down and convince you."

"I'm glad Ryder is to be with you."

"He is. And maybe even the others will find help and strength in being on their own."

"Doesn't Ryder have a staff-teaching position in St. Louis?"

"He does. He is going to resign, effective in six months."

"Then he's coming back here. That's good. You'll need help."

"He's not entirely unselfish. He wants to come. It seems there is a girl here. A young woman."

Clancy looked alarmed and bothered.

"The only drawback," Webbe continued quietly, "is that she, too, has money."

Clancy frowned, then he began to smile. "Susan?" he asked. "Oh, that would be great! Except . . ."

"What?"

"Can we keep that secret too, for a time? Because, with Gretchen, Susan is my ace in the hole. You see, I took over Sue's husband's practice. I spend some time with her on estate matters . . ."

"And Gretchen, with crumbs on her chin, reaches out for the rest of the cake."

"She does. It keeps her near the table. I mean . . ."

"We seem able to know what each of us means. But I am glad you are pleased about Ryder and Susan. There's no formal engagement—but both are interested. It was their reason not to go to Gretchen's party at Lucky Peak. They had other plans."

"I can believe that. Does Susan know about the foundation?"

"Only that Ryder expects to return here to work. By the time he does come—he'll be dropping in on us frequently, I imagine—the project can be announced."

"Wheee!" said Clancy. "What a year I'll put in. Keeping all this from Greta will be the hardest job."

"You'll do it. You know, I accepted the position here

because I'd met you as a member of the hospital board, and you would be available to help me. I had already scouted the general location."

"You would have."

"I hope we can get quietly to work."

"Could you plan to spend a week, solid, in my office?"

Webbe laughed. "I'm a doctor. You're the legal light. And in your first contract, so specify."

"Oh, I shall, I shall!"

"You've already been a great help. You've squashed the thing that Linda tried to start."

"And saved Holt's hide. Really, he doesn't half know what he has to be grateful for where you are concerned. This foundation will be a big thing for his city."

"Yes, it will be. There will be referral contacts with medical centers all across the country, and out of it. Something like the liver-transplant work in Denver. But I'm glad to help this town. I like it, and the people."

"And that was why you came here."

Dr. Webbe smiled a bit wryly. "I came here for peace and quiet," he said.

Clancy laughed.

"They're still here," said the doctor. "I hope."

Clancy nodded. "We hope."

Webbe sat on for an hour after Clancy had departed. ". . . Late for dinner," he had said. "Gretchen will scalp me. And she's sure to detect that I am keeping a secret from her."

"I don't think we should tell anyone, prematurely."

"We should not. But with that suspicion in her mind, she's going to stick close, Doctor. Very close, and watchful."

Mac sat on, watching the sunset sky. Then he went to the hospital and made surgery rounds. Afterward, wearing a sweater, he was back on the patio, stretched out in the long chair, gazing at the stars which seemed very close at hand, and large, when Ryder came home from his date with Susan.

"Hey!" he cried. "Shouldn't you be in bed? I see that you have surgery scheduled for eight tomorrow."

"I do. Groin hernia surgery on a seven-year-old boy. I promised I wouldn't make a really big hole in him. So I'll move inside soon. But I had some thinking to do."

"I'll bet you've been doing it, too. That's how I located you. I could hear the wheels turning. Did you have dinner?"

"I picked something up in the diet kitchen when I made bed check."

"Soft or low-residue?"

His father chuckled. "I don't like their high-protein supplements," he confessed. "The substitute steak tastes like blotters. I've made a note never to get sick."

"Did you talk to Clancy?" Ryder sat down.

"Oh, yes, indeed. He is on top of things. He's decided on a consultant legal firm already familiar with foundation work, and he plans to have a Denver construction company bid on our building. It built their house."

"You couldn't do better, probably."

In the half light, his father's eyeglasses flashed. "He says Gretchen will be so intrigued by the secret she'll know he is keeping that there's no danger of her getting into other mischief. Like following you to St. Louis."

"Oh, she wouldn't do that."

"She told me she was thinking about it. You must have

a fateful effect on women. I believed her enough that I promised myself I would help keep her in line."

"You won't count on Clancy's being able to handle that?"

"I want him to put all his strength and ability on my job. But, yes, he does seem able to handle the girl. I don't think she knows he does it, or even that she needs handling. But Clancy is one of the strong ones . . ."

"And very much in love with her."

"Yes. Oh, yes, he is."

"She's quite a girl."

"Though her parents spoiled her and weakened her."

Ryder laughed. "I know your philosophy. The strong must help the weak. But I dispute your claim that Gretchen is weak."

"I didn't say feeble. And I expected you to dispute me. There are those who do not think your mother is weak. But she is, and she needs help."

"What do you expect you'll have to do for her just now? You didn't buy this small house with her in mind."

"No, I didn't. She has the place in Baltimore. She loves to travel—"

"Without a passport."

"Yeah. But there's still Mexico, Canada, Hawaii, the Virgin Islands . . . This whole country. She'll come home, even here perhaps, and plan the next trip. Then return, and plan again. I don't expect she's ever a real social success where she goes, because she has this complex about people abusing her."

"If she comes here, couldn't she make trouble for you?"

"Probably. And I won't like it, probably. But, Ryder,

I understand there was a bit of trouble in the original Eden."

Ryder laughed and stood up. "I think we should go in to bed."

Mac rose and followed his son. "You know," he said, "her weakness was why I married your mother in the first place. Now I have her, Linda, and Tom."

"And me."

"Well, there's nothing weak about you!"

They went to each of the two bedrooms. As they prepared for bed, they talked back and forth across the narrow hall. Both men were setting out clothing for the next day, in the way of doctors, before undressing.

"Who looks after us big strong guys?" Ryder called.

"No one."

"Dad . . ." Ryder came into his room. "Are you really sure you want me to come and work with you here?"

Mac frowned a little. "I'm sure about my wanting you," he said. "How about you? I want you only if *you* want to do it."

Ryder leaned against the door frame, gazing at his father.

"I've always hoped," said Webbe slowly, "that you and I could work together. But, better than that, would be for you to work someplace, anyplace, and make a good life for yourself. Find yourself a grand girl . . ."

"I think I have found her, Dad. But how does a guy really know?"

"He doesn't. You won't. About his work, and about the girl. But in any case, if it doesn't seem to work out, make it work, son. Make it work! Don't run away. As I've done."

"How did you run? Where did you run?"

"I buried myself in my medical work. I left you kids and my wife to go your own ways. Then when my mistakes promised to catch up with me, I came out here . . ."

"Mhmmmn. I don't think many would consider what you're planning to be a running-away. Even what you've done this past year. I am told you sweat blood putting the hospital on its feet."

"I haven't sweat any blood. And I think I have done some good work. I haven't failed too much, even with Gretchen . . ."

"Susan says that Clancy has abandoned his job with Gretchen, that he lets her do as she pleases, just as her parents did."

"I think Susan is wrong. They are building their life together. I'll bet when she married Clancy, people said she would ruin the young man."

"Maybe you would have said that, too."

"Probably. But now—I predict that Gretchen will be a great woman by the time she's—oh, maybe by the time she's forty!"

Ryder laughed. "And a great doctor, too?"

"Not great, maybe. Anyway, in my crystal ball, motherhood comes through more clearly."

"Fair enough, though I don't think you're giving Gretchen herself enough consideration."

"Maybe not."

"She and I— And if I leave, there is sure to be some other man."

"Possibly," said Webbe. "Even me."

This startled his son. His face showed that he was

considering what he would do if that should happen. "It certainly would set out a different pot of stew," he said thoughtfully.

His father laughed. "Yes, it would," he agreed. "But I think I'll stick with the stew I put on the fire this afternoon."

"I hope so. I like Gretchen, and I think she's made a good marriage. I'd stand ready to let her be lucky there."

"That should do it," said Mac. "I'm going to shower."

Things went as he and Clancy had hoped they would, as they had planned the course of events. Ryder left at the end of the week, saying to all interested only that he was going back to work. But he did promise Susan that he would return.

"My dad may need me. His name can't stay buried, and already cases are being brought to him from Portland, Seattle— He can't resist a crippled infant. I stand ready to take on his job as Chief of Staff."

That was all even Susan was to know.

As for Gretchen—

CHAPTER 14

GRETCHEN was at work in the hospital. "He's a slave driver," she complained to Clancy.

"Who is?"

"McKinney Webbe is who."

"I thought you wanted him to teach you practical medicine."

"I am having second thoughts about that."

Clancy said nothing, nor did Dr. Webbe when Gretchen offered her protests to him.

He was stern, but he was also courteous to her, and considerate, up to a point. He took her off pediatrics and assigned her to a full schedule in surgery. She was to assist as needed, but to be ready in any case. Dr. Shaw never needed her. Dr. Webbe always did. He was operating that morning, three or four days after Ryder left. O.r. was very busy, with green-robed, capped doctors and nurses standing shoulder to shoulder around the table. Gretchen was afraid of surgery, but admitted to herself that she forgot her fears when Mac was operating.

"I never saw such hands!" she told the scrub nurse.

"He operates with the skin of his fingers! And never bungles or smears."

"He's delicate. His touch, I mean."

"Yes, he is. But he doesn't think much of my sewing."

The nurse laughed, and went out of the locker room. Gretchen put on her white coat and went out, too, wondering why Dr. Webbe had asked her to meet him in Recovery.

She soon found out. He asked her to gown and come in, he asked her to check the patient on whom they had just operated. He carefully watched her as she wrote on the chart.

"All right," he said. "Come across to the desk."

There he sat down, but left her standing. "I have made out a schedule for you, Dr. Cobbins," he said formally. "With expected day-to-day changes, this should keep you busy for the rest of this year."

"This year" had reached only April. Gretchen swiftly read the page he had handed to her. She looked up in protest, her eyes wide. "This is a killer!" she declared.

"You said you wanted to learn."

"Yes, I did. But . . ."

"I can't take you by the hand and lead you step by step. The best I can do is to set up a schedule for you, and arrange for it to be followed. If it is followed, by the end of this year you will have learned enough for me to be able to say you have done your intern work, and are ready for resident duty."

"But . . ."

"I have asked Dr. Fielder to come back on limited duty, and to serve as your teaching resident. Your supervisory resident."

"Acupuncture," said Gretchen darkly.

Dr. Webbe smiled. "Dr. Fielder is old, and has his peculiarities. About things like the diet of admitted patients."

"Soft diet for a broken toe!"

"It doesn't hurt the patient. Fielder is a good, conscientious doctor, and he will know if what you do is right or wrong."

"And report to you."

"I'll read his reports, yes. I am Chief of Staff."

Yes. He was.

Gretchen studied the schedule again. Dr. Webbe was taking a telephone call. "Yes," she heard him say, "I am sure Dr. Cobbins will have time to stop in this evening. As a matter of practice, we do not arrange house calls, but we do make some exceptions. She will be able to tell if Mrs. Callier should be admitted to the hospital."

Gretchen was making gestures and whispering loud "no's" into his ear.

He put the phone down and lifted an eyebrow to Gretchen.

"I won't go to Ida B.'s," she told him.

"The old lady has fallen and injured her leg. Her niece . . ."

"Her niece asked for me to come. It's a trick, Doctor. I have been avoiding those two for some time. I won't even go to parties where I suspect they will be present. . . ."

"This is not a party invitation, Gretchen. It is a professional call. I expect you to go."

"And attend her if she does need hospitalization?" She sounded like a sulky child.

"Not unless she needs surgery. You are now on surgical duty." He rose from the chart desk. "Come down to my office," he said.

"Dr. Webbe," said Gretchen as they walked along the corridor—the chief was still in his scrub suit and cap—"was it I who asked you to teach me, or my husband?"

"It was you. Though Clancy did say that you wanted to learn. He thought you did want that."

"Ye-es. If I worked at the hospital at all. But he would rather I did not."

Dr. Webbe let her precede him into his office. He opened the blinds and stood for a minute, admiring the view of the sun on the snow-covered mountaintops. "Did he have alternative plans for you, Gretchen?" he asked.

"Well, yes, he did. I could begin a family. A big family. Neither of us wants a single child. And then I myself thought—" She broke off. She would not mention Susan Warrington and the good chance that Clancy could transfer his attention to *her*.

"A family," said Webbe thoughtfully, pouring coffee from a carafe into two mugs. "That will take a little time. Meanwhile"—he indicated the schedule which she still held in her hands—"we'll get to work."

Gretchen sat down in the chair beside his desk, and drank some coffee.

"Dr. Webbe," she said, "do you know how Dolly Int-Veld died? I know you and Jonah have become friends."

"Yes, we have. I like him very much. And he has told me about his wife."

"Yes. We were his friends, too. When she had that stroke, Dr. Shaw thought, and has said many times since, that I did wrong not to agree that he should do immediate surgery on her. I was her doctor of record. That was before I became an intern." She looked up and smiled at the Chief, who was regarding her with his customary alert gravity.

"Do you think he could have done it?" she asked. "Shaw?"

"Do you think he would have?"

"Yes. Oh, yes!"

"He's not a neurosurgeon."

"No, but she might have lived. We lost six hours getting in a specialist."

"But that specialist *was* a neurosurgeon."

"I know. But it was that case which made me tell Clancy I wanted to learn the things I needed to know."

"All right, Gretchen. Now I'll teach you a very important thing. We doctors cannot second-guess on cases. As of that moment, you exercised your best judgment."

"Shaw says I was prejudiced against him. And I admit that I was."

"Yes, I've known that. I also have watched Shaw work. And he definitely is not a neurosurgeon. His capabilities are limited, and I do limit his performance. I doubt if my predecessor, Dr. Wagner, whom I know you admired, would have opened Dolly's skull."

"Would you?"

He laughed. "You're second-guessing again."

She stood up. "I'll never become any kind of surgeon!" she told him firmly. "Not after watching you."

He nodded. "I'd settle if you will just learn to retract," he said calmly. He began to look at the papers on his desk.

She watched him. "It doesn't make any difference to you, does it, that I've told you that I admire you? Maybe *admire* isn't strong enough . . ."

He reached his hand for the telephone. "Oh, get to work!" he said in exasperation. He spoke into the phone and put it down. "We both should keep busy!" he told her. "I should, I know. I have this hospital to run, and the things I want to do about my house. Have you seen my swimming pool? I'll never know how Ryder got it installed within a month, though it's still little more than a tiled hole in the ground. My house is furnished, but there are still things to be done there. My wife will be joining me soon." He did not look up at Gretchen. "You'll be getting pregnant," he swept along. "You—"

"Do you think," she asked curiously, "that getting—that having a family will satisfy me?"

"Well, that's up to you, Gretchen. Loving Clancy should be enough for most women."

"And there's no time for living, is there?"

He smiled somewhat wryly. "Somehow," he said, "the living and the loving, it gets done."

"Yes, I suppose it does. Sometimes in a roundabout way. Til Holt says Clancy is a lucky man, even with a wife like me."

"I'll agree with him. Was he in love with Kathy? Til?"

"He knew he could not marry a lush . . ."

"That took strength. I admire him for it."

"If we could get her dried out . . ."

"You could work on that."

She shook the paper in her hand. "With all this you've planned for me?" she asked. She rose, took a step, and laid the paper on his desk. "I was going to tell you," she said. "I'm going to have to quit this career anyway."

"To have a child."

"I may be able to work that in, too . . ."

"Gretchen, are you afraid of motherhood?"

"Sure, sure," she answered readily. "Only the silly girls of sixteen aren't afraid of that. That's why they get into it so easily. With me—I don't like failure."

"You won't fail. You'll be a great mother. Your girls will want to be like you, and your boys will adore you."

She flushed, but shook her head. "I hope," she said. "But there's another thing. Did you know that Delmo Lorella, my deaf-mute housekeeper, had had a stroke?"

"No! I did not know! When did this happen?"

"Last week. She's been here that long."

"I must have missed something."

"Oh, she's on medical. Dr. Lovett's patient."

Their new internist. Yes.

"I may have seen her in passing—even read her chart, without realizing . . ."

"Yes. She seems to be doing all right. But her right side was affected and she has no use of that hand. Since she is deaf and mute, she can't communicate."

Dr. Webbe rubbed his hand back over his hair. "Oh, dear!"

"Yes. Stephen and I talk to her in sign. Clancy was beginning to learn. But she can't do more than blink at us. In time, Lovett thinks she can write . . ."

Dr. Webbe got out of his chair and walked to the window. "I've been busy," he said. "Too busy!"

"Yes. I know you spent a day with Clancy. And right after that, you disappeared for a whole afternoon."

Dr. Webbe glanced at her. "This is shocking!" he said.

"I have never given any thought to that sort of development for a deaf person."

"No, I hadn't, either. But—since she's been taking care of me, my house, and my husband, I feel that now I must take care of those things for her. She'll be coming home in a day or two, and will live in their trailer. But I must take her place in our house. Stephen will help tremendously, of course. I hope I can make her know this is something I want to do."

Dr. Webbe came to her and put his hands on her shoulders. "You're all right, Gretchen," he said warmly. "And you're not anywhere close to being forty years old."

She looked at him questioningly.

"Just a bet I had with Ryder," he said.

Gretchen shrugged. "I'm probably not all right, either," she said, "though if I ever am, it probably won't show. But—I'll try."

Mac went back to his desk and sat down. He tore the "schedule" into bits and dropped it into the wastebasket. "When I first came here," he said, "I asked you why you had married Clancy." He saw the color rise in her face. "And, since, I've heard about that silly boast you made. But now I want to know the real reason." He waited.

"You'd first have to know the sort of girl I was then," she said slowly. "Demanding. Too possessive. So I either devoured men, or drove them away."

"Til Holt?"

"Yes. I knew, and hoped, I would one day meet a man who would put up with me."

"Clancy?"

She smiled. "I'm beginning to think so. And through his love and patience, I am beginning to change. Until

I married him, and since, I have worked. A little. And I've been free. But now . . . I really like Clancy!" she said earnestly. "But we just seem to go along. Happy enough, I suppose. He's fun to be with, and I like to do the things he likes to do. But I have wondered if I did trick him into marrying me."

"*Clancy?*"

"Yes."

"Do you really think you could, Gretchen?"

"Well, I've managed—with other men—"

"Clancy is *not* other men!"

"No. He isn't."

"You're damn lucky to have him," said the Chief, sounding angry. "You should hang onto him, anyway you can. Like telling him you love him. Telling yourself . . ."

Gretchen nodded. "I know, and I'll try."

"He loves you. And now I'll give you my last bit of instruction, Doctor. Gleaned from a very busy life of my own. Don't think of love," he said, "so much in terms of passion as of tenderness. If young people could be made to learn that! If you can. Give more thought and expression to the adult needs of affection, my dear, of sympathy with your man, and regard for him."

Gretchen nodded. "Thank you, Doctor. Clancy already knows that lesson."

"Then you'll make do." He turned back to his papers.

But Gretchen did not leave. "Do I still have to go see Ida B.?" she asked.

"Who?"

"Mrs. Callier."

"Oh, yes. Why, yes, of course you do, Gretchen. Of course you do!"